RED LIGHT, GREEN LIGHT

ARE YOU GAME?

RHIAN CAHILL

DEDICATION

For those of us with fond memories of childhood games.
And for Mr. Summers for his advice and Eden Summers for asking.

1

West's gaze connected with the woman across the room for what seemed like the millionth time in the last hour. Since he'd arrived, she'd avoided him with everything except those mesmerizing eyes of hers. It wasn't the first time they'd played this game. Only lately, he'd grown tired of playing—their constant game of red light, green light felt anything but fun. Especially when the light was red more than it was green.

He'd walked away from her once. Young and stupid, he hadn't really thought about what he was giving up when he didn't make a move beyond their one night. And by the time he *had* figured it out, he was too late. She was dating someone else. That was one mistake he didn't need to repeat to learn from.

"Shit, man. Tell me you are not seriously thinking of going there?" His best friend elbowed him in the ribs.

Bringing his beer to his mouth, West took a sip—his eyes still locked on Kelsey—before he turned to face Zac. "Going where?" He'd play dumb if he had to.

Zac arched one eyebrow. "Dude. I know that look. It says, 'I wanna fuck you'."

West grinned. "Thanks, but no thanks. You know I don't swing that way."

"Fuck off." Zac elbowed him again, this time with a little more force. "You know I'm talking about Kelsey. You don't wanna go there."

Too late. Been there, done that. Should never have moved on.

But West wasn't about to tell his best friend that train had already departed. Ten years ago. Turning back to look at Kels, West caught her eye once more and sent her a wink.

"Shit. She's giving you the look now." Zac took a swig of his beer and choked. "Fuck." He wiped his mouth with the back of his hand. "That's not the I-want-to-do-you look. That's the I've-done-you-and-I-want-to-do-you-again look." Zac rounded on him and got in his face. "What the fuck, West?"

Crap. West took another sip of beer as he turned away from the woman of his dreams to lean his elbows on the bar. He had to be careful. Too many words would reveal something he didn't want anyone, including his best friend, to know. Too little would prompt questions he had no intention of answering. "What? She's hot. I'm not dead and it's not like there's a law against looking." He shrugged and tried to portray a nonchalant attitude when he felt anything but indifferent when it came to Kelsey.

"Yes, there is." Zac got right in his face again. "She was married to Bry."

"*Was* being the operative word." And West didn't need to be reminded. He'd spent three years of his life living that particular nightmare. Not to mention the three Kelsey had dated Bryan before becoming Mrs. Newman.

"Jesus. Are you for real?" Zac glanced around before lowering his voice. "You've already gone there, haven't you? Are you the reason she filed for divorce?"

Shit. He wished. No, Kels and Bry had done that all on their own without outside help. And from what Kelsey had told him—and what seemed to be common opinion among their group—it had been a long time coming. West was the first to acknowledge they never should have gotten married. Not when he knew Bry didn't want

Kelsey the way he did. No one could want her on the level West did. His bones ached he wanted her so badly. Of course, he'd had her.

Once.

Okay, more than once, but it had only been one night. One night of absolute pleasure his body had spent the last ten years craving a repeat of. He shook his head clear of memories that had the power to bring him to his knees and focused on the present.

"C'mon, Zac, you have to admit she's smokin'." West took another swig of beer.

"Sure. But which one of our group isn't? Every woman we went to school with is hot enough to melt the South Pole. Must have been something in the water that year." Zac grinned and West joined him, hoping he was pulling off the blasé attitude of a guy checking out a passing woman.

Heat and movement behind him had West glancing over his shoulder then jack-knifing upright and around, tightening his fingers on the bottle in his hand.

Kelsey.

"Hey, Kels, how ya doing?" West played it cool like he always did when he was around this woman.

"Good." She smiled and West's insides clenched, his pulse racing with heated blood.

He'd had those lips wrapped around his cock. Knew how hot and wet her mouth was. How hard she could suck.

"Thanks for helping me move my stuff the other day."

Her words brought him out of the past and back to the crowded bar. "Oh, right. No worries. Any time."

He was conscious of Zac standing statue-still beside him. Silence settled between the three of them and West knew he needed to say something to break the tension before the moment turned awkward. His gaze landed on Kelsey's empty wine glass and he latched on to the diversion. "You want another drink?"

Kels looked at the glass in her hand and shook her head. "No, I've already had too many. I'm going to have to leave my car in town as it is, don't need a hangover tomorrow to add to the inconvenience."

West put his bottle on the bar behind him. "I'll drive your car home if you want. I've only had one and I caught a ride in with Zac." He took the glass from her hand. "Consider me your designated driver."

"Really? That would be great. I've got an early class tomorrow so I was going to have to get a cab back into town at some ungodly hour." She smiled up at him and West's insides did that whole clenching thing again. Only this time, his groin tightened to the point of pain.

"You still teaching those community-college classes?" Zac asked. It was the first words he'd spoken since Kels had come over and West had pretty much forgotten he was there.

"Yeah. Tomorrow is budgets for the elderly. I think the youngest member of class is sixty-five." She smiled.

Kels had been working at their local community college since the day she'd received her accounting degree. She did it for free, and West knew it had been a bone of contention between her and Bry their whole married life. He was glad she hadn't bowed to Bry's demands to either be paid or stop giving the classes. Another reason he'd known the two of them were wrong for each other. Bry just didn't get Kelsey's need to help those without the means to help themselves.

"Oh, there's Coop. I wanna catch him before he leaves." Zac was gone before either of them could say a word.

"Did I scare him off?" Kels asked.

"No. He was a little uncomfortable with our exchange of glances earlier." West shrugged. "Not our problem."

"Did he say anything?" Anxiety pinched her mouth and turned her blue eyes a shade darker than normal.

"Nothing you should be worried about."

She narrowed her eyes at him.

"Honest, Kels, its fine." He brushed his hand against the back of hers.

Kelsey jerked away and, eyes wide, glanced either side of them to see if anyone had noticed the intimate caress. "Um, I'd like to get out of here early, if that's okay? Would you mind leaving in about thirty minutes? If not, I can go back to my original plan and get a cab home."

West sighed. Just like that, they were back on the friend's side of the fence. He couldn't count the number of times they'd skirted the line of friendship in the last three years. He'd hoped to be closer to her by now. Hoped they'd have found a way to cross the line from friends to lovers now that she was free. "Whenever you're ready to go," he said with a tight smile.

She returned his smile with one that didn't quite reach her eyes. He hated that smile. It was the one she used when she was trying to pretend everything was okay when it wasn't. He'd seen that facade far too many times in the past and he couldn't stand to see it right now. Not aimed at him.

"I'm gonna go sit with the guys." West indicated the table where Zac had run off to. "Come get me when you're ready to leave."

West didn't run, but he may as well have. He needed to think. Kelsey had been the girl he'd lost his virginity with. The one he'd let walk away and hook up with a friend. He'd wanted her to be happy and thought Bry might be able to do that. Except Bry hadn't, and West had spent ten years of his life sitting on the sidelines while the woman he loved wasn't really happy. It'd cut him to the core to stand back and do nothing. It still did. But he was done with the sideline.

He glanced back in Kelsey's direction. He was getting in the game.

West wasn't sure how or when he made the decision, but he was going after Kels and was prepared to break every friend code there was to claim her as his.

KELSEY LEANED her forehead against the stall door as she turned the latch. It was getting harder and harder to control her reactions around West. She'd snuck away from the group to hide out in the bathroom for a much needed breather. He didn't need to touch her to get her motor revving. Just one look from those stormy-gray eyes sent her pulse racing and her nerves into a frenzy. But the second he'd run his fingers over her skin... God, she'd almost melted at his feet.

The outer door opened and voices echoed as heels clicked over the tiled floor. She straightened and stepped back, glancing over her shoulder to check the toilet lid was closed before taking a seat. Leaning her elbows on her knees and propping her head in her hands, she stared at the floor.

What the hell was she going to do about West? They couldn't keep this up. *She* couldn't keep it up. At some point, she'd break, and as much as she wanted to cross that line with him, she equally feared it.

She'd tangled herself up with West before and all she'd gotten was a night of unforgettable pleasure and a broken heart. It had taken her a year to get over West's rejection. They'd never discussed what had happened between them. Not once in all the years since had he brought it up. Then again, neither had she. And yet their sizzling chemistry had continued to bubble beneath the surface of their platonic friendship even during her ill-fated marriage to one of his best friends.

She groaned. God she'd made a mess of her and Bry's marriage. She'd loved Bryan. Still loved him. But not the way a wife should. Not with everything she was. How could she when she'd given a huge piece of her heart to the boy she'd given her virginity to? If she were honest—and she should be, at least with herself—West had owned her heart long before they'd made their pact to divest each other of their virginity.

Kelsey had no one to blame but herself for the hurt she'd suffered afterwards. She'd gone into that night with her eyes wide open, but like every other teenage girl with stars in her eyes and dreams in her heart, she'd thought loving him physically would unlock his heart and he wouldn't be able to live another day without her. She shook her head at how naive she'd been. How she'd allowed visions of fairy-tale-style happy ever after to cloud her mind and render her defense-less—vulnerable.

After their night, West had ignored her to the point that Kelsey had thought she'd done something wrong—something to turn him off. For months, she'd gone over and over every second she'd spent in his arms until she'd come to the only conclusion she could. He didn't want *her*. It wasn't as though he'd jumped straight from her bed to someone else's. He'd been without a significant other until long after she'd begun dating Bry. Not that she'd really seen much of West in the year following their one night.

They'd both been busy with university and work. Kelsey knew she'd avoided more than one event West had been at because seeing him and not being able to touch him had cut so deep she'd struggled to keep tears at bay. She'd skipped out early on a lot of their friends' birthdays in those first few months.

"Hey." The door rattled as someone thumped on the other side. "You about done in there?"

"Give me a sec," Kelsey called out as she pushed to her feet. She turned around and flushed the toilet even though she hadn't used it. Unlocking the door, she kept her gaze lowered and made her way to the sink where two women were in the middle of a whispered discussion.

Kelsey froze when she overheard Zac's name, but when she tried to inch a little closer to hear more clearly, they turned her way. She quickly leaned towards the mirror and fluffed her hair, pretending she was oblivious to them and what they were saying. Getting caught eavesdropping on what was intended to be a private conversation wouldn't be the best of circumstances. When the woman closest to her stepped in her direction, Kelsey figured she'd managed to put herself in that exact situation.

"Oh, hey. Don't you hang out with Zachary Moreland and that group of hunks?" the woman asked.

Kelsey turned and had to stifle a gasp. Had she thought they were women? Neither of them could be a day over nineteen. They had to be at least eighteen to get into the bar, but Kelsey had a suspicion they'd barely scraped past that milestone. "Um, which guys?" Stalling seemed to be her best option.

"The one's hanging out in the back of the bar. I saw you talking with Zachary and another one earlier." Blondie nudged her equally blonde friend. "You did too, right?"

Kelsey sighed. If she had a dollar for every time some strange female asked her about one of the guys, she'd be richer than Midas. "Yeah, I know them." She turned to leave.

"Could you introduce us?"

Kelsey's eyes popped wide and her mouth dropped open as she spun back towards the teenagers. Well, that was a first. No one had been brave enough to ask for an introduction before. "I don't think so. For a start, I don't even know who you are."

"I'm Candy—" the blonde who'd done all the talking so far waved at her friend, "—and this is Missy."

What kind of names were those? Kelsey shook her head. "Sorry. No can do."

Before either of them could say another word, Kelsey strode around them and out the door. She'd taken no more than five steps along the dark hallway when a large shadow pushed off the wall into her path. A shaft of fear shot up her spine before she recognized West.

"Oh, it's you." She placed a hand on her chest over her thumping heart.

"Hey, you okay?" He stepped in front of her, the tips of his shoes bare inches from hers. "You were in there a long time."

West was right. She had been in there a while, and Kelsey shouldn't be surprised that he'd come to check on her. Regardless of their strained friendship, he'd always watched out for her. Then again, maybe it was just her who felt the tension between them. "I'm fine."

"You sure? We can head out now if you're feeling under the weather." He bent forward so he could look directly into her eyes.

Kelsey smiled. "Is that a polite way of asking if I've had too much to drink?" She and every one of her friends knew she was a lightweight when it came to alcohol.

West moved closer, his white teeth flashing as he smiled down at her. "You and I both know it only takes a couple of glasses to put you under the table."

Returning his smile, she was about to reply when someone slammed into her from behind, shoving her against him. Kelsey threw her hands out to catch herself. They landed on his chest as he spanned his hands around her waist to steady her.

"Thanks for nothing, bitch," Candy muttered as she and Missy pushed past in the narrow corridor.

"Hey!" West glanced over his shoulder as the women disappeared out of sight. Turning back to Kelsey, he asked, "What was that about?"

"You don't want to know." He arched one eyebrow. Then again, maybe he did. "Fine. But don't let it go to your head. They wanted me to introduce them to our group. Well, you guys anyway."

His other eyebrow shot up his forehead. "Why? Who are they?"

"I haven't a clue who they are, and isn't it obvious why?" Kelsey would never understand how none of the guys had figured out their appeal to the opposite sex and used it to get laid. In fact, she couldn't recall any of them having anything other than serious relationships. All of them were standup guys who didn't indulge in one-night stands. Unless they'd managed to keep their sexual exploits well hidden, but she didn't think so. While they weren't inclined to share their conquests with her, she'd never overheard any of them bragging about women and never seen them hook up whenever they were all out together.

"You don't know them?"

She shook her head. "Nope."

"Wow. That takes balls."

Kelsey laughed. "I think it was balls they were after."

"Jeez." He let go of her waist and cupped one elbow. "C'mon, let's get back to the table to warn everyone."

"Why warn them? They're big boys, I'm sure they can take care of themselves." Kelsey tugged her arm from his grasp and moved a step in front before they entered the main room of the bar.

"A couple have had a few too many, and with vultures like that hanging around, someone's bound to get themselves in trouble."

West placed his hand on her lower back and steered her through the crowd. The place had gotten busier while she'd been hiding in the bathroom. It didn't help that their group had taken up residence all the way in the back of the room.

"Hey, we're heading out now. Anyone want a lift?" West asked when they reached the table. After a no from everyone, he scanned the area, spotted the two women from the bathroom and nodded his head in their general direction. "Blonde and blonder in the far corner are on the prowl. Don't anyone be stupid."

Zac glanced over and paled. "Shit. Again?"

"You know them?" Kelsey asked.

Zac let out a gush of air and slouched down in his seat. "Yeah, worst luck. Blonder—I think her name is something stupid like Lolli—is the younger sister of that footballer who was in the papers a few months ago. You know the one up on assault charges."

Kelsey laughed. "It's Candy, but I guess Lolli is close."

"What?" Zac asked.

"She introduced herself in the bathroom when she recognized me as someone who'd been talking to you."

Zac's mouth hung open.

"How the hell do you know her?" West asked Zac.

"She came into the office with her brother every damn time he met with his lawyers. Barely legal and on the hunt for a sugar daddy that one."

By now, all the guys had craned their necks for a better look, and Kelsey wasn't surprised when Blonder—Candy—headed in their direction, her friend trailing behind.

"Shit," West muttered when he saw what Kelsey was looking at. "We're outta here. Catch you all later."

Kelsey barely managed a goodbye over her shoulder when West spun around and towed her across the room.

2

W est pulled into Kelsey's driveway and killed the engine. The drive had been filled with mundane chatter about work and of course her usual nagging about his need for an office manager. He'd been fighting her on that for months now, but truth be told, she was right. He needed someone in the office full-time because the hours he put in on paperwork around everything else he did weren't cutting it anymore. But if he had to have anyone poking around the innards of Weston's, he wanted Kelsey. And she refused to take the job.

He slipped the key from the ignition and opened his door. He had one foot on the ground when Kels grabbed his arm and stopped him from getting out.

"What are you doing?" she asked, her voice a little high—a little tight.

"Getting out."

"Why?" She dug her fingers into his forearm.

Okay. This was interesting. "Um, because we're at your house?"

"Yes, but you don't have to come in."

West arched an eyebrow at her obvious horror at the thought of him coming inside. "I wasn't planning to come in, Kels. But I don't plan on sitting in your car all night either."

"Oh. Right." She licked her lips and West was hit with the urge to lean over and follow her tongue with his. "Okay. I'll see you later then."

Before he could make sense of the conversation, or her fear, she was out of the car and hurrying along the footpath. "What the hell?" he mumbled as he climbed out of the car and, shaking his head, shut the door behind him. Unlike Kels, West took his time walking to her door.

She'd stopped on the path, her hand stretched out in his direction, her gaze directed at the ground. "I need my house key."

He'd figured as much, but she'd jumped out of the car before he could hand over her key ring. West wasn't sure what had her so flustered, but she was as twitchy as a cat in a room full of rocking chairs.

He held out her keys.

She snatched them from him before she turned on her heel and launched herself up the step. Except her shoe clipped the edge and she tipped forward, quickly on her way to meeting the floor with her face. West lunged for her and managed to grab her shirt. In a split second, he realized he couldn't stop her fall with his limited hold. With a hard yank, he pulled her towards him. The action spun her around and brought her close enough for him to wrap his other arm around her waist.

He pulled her against him. Bracketing her torso with his arms, West hauled her up until her chest was flush with his and her feet dangled above the ground. Her body went taut as air rushed from her lungs like a punctured balloon. In this position, they were eye to eye, and he took in her expression. Fear and shock filled her gaze before another emotion overtook them. She sucked in a deep breath and her breasts rose to press against him. West didn't miss the hard points of her nipples digging in to him.

"Kels." Her name was no more than a breath, and in the next second, he ditched all common sense and slanted his mouth over hers.

She didn't fight him like he expected. Instead, she melted into him. She thrust her tongue out to stroke over his and he took the unspoken invitation to explore. Memories bombarded him. Images of her naked beneath him. Of his mouth and hands searching out every sensitive spot on her lithe body. Except she wasn't the same as before. There were new curves, new slopes, and West struggled to control the need to rip her clothes off and discover every one of them.

West moaned when she slid her hands over his shoulders and up his neck until her fingertips tangled in his hair. It was a little long, in need of a trim, but right now, with Kels tugging on the ends, West vowed to never cut it again if she just kept up the sexy pull. His groin throbbed as blood rushed to fill his cock with heat. The sweet ache he always felt around Kels exploded into a blinding flash of pain that singed his insides.

He had to have her.

Had to bury himself so deep nobody could tell them apart.

A growl rumbled in his chest as he gripped her arse and pressed his hard length into her. The way he held her meant they were lined up perfectly, and he took the single step to her porch without looking. He kept going until he had her trapped between his body and her front door.

Timber rattled and Kels tore her mouth from his. He saw the second the lust haze cleared. The second she realized what they were doing and where they were doing it. He'd never forced himself on a woman, and he wouldn't be starting with this one no matter how much he craved her. So when she shoved her hands against his shoulders and wiggled in his arms, he slipped his hands to her hips, took a step back and lowered her to the floor. It took strength he didn't know he had to let go of her completely.

Her mouth worked. Opened. Closed. Only nothing came out, and West couldn't think of one damn word to say either. Well, none that weren't about getting naked and continuing inside. It took him a moment of dragging in deep breaths to clear his head, but once he did, he knew there was no way they were going to finish what they'd started. He could see the big red light she'd turned on. Kels didn't need to say a word, it was written all over her face, blazed in her sky-blue eyes.

That one taste was all he was getting tonight, and unless he wanted to start an argument and push her farther away, he had to suck it up and keep his raging lust in check. Glancing at her hands, he saw she no longer held her keys. He turned around and spotted them lying on the path. She must have dropped them while they were locked at the lips. With a grimace of pain, West leapt off the single step and bent to scoop up her key ring. The tight fit of his jeans wasn't kind to the full-blown hard-on he sported.

Hiding his discomfort behind a smile, he turned and headed back to her door. He made quick work of sliding the key into the lock and swinging the door wide before pressing the keys into her hand. If he was going to do the right thing and leave, he had to do it now.

"I'll catch you later." He gripped her elbow and urged her inside. West tried not to laugh at the shell-shocked look on her face, but he couldn't hold back the smile curling his lips. "See you Monday."

"M-monday?"

"Yep. Tax time, remember?" The look of horror that passed over her face made him chuckle. "Does that look mean I'm in for a bill other than yours?"

"What? Oh no. I'd forgotten all about our meeting, that's all."

He'd just bet she had. After that kiss, West was lucky to remember his name. He smiled and leaned into the house, making her jump back a step. But she needn't worry, he wasn't about to touch her again. Not tonight. "Lock the door."

West pulled the door closed and waited for the deadlock to click into place before he left. Good thing it was a ten-minute walk home. He thought about running the distance to disperse some of the energy buzzing in his veins. But a walk in the cold night air would help cool him off. Plus, he had a lot of thinking and planning to do. She may have been on board with their kiss, but the second sanity had returned, she'd backed right away without moving a step. They'd been building up to that kiss for months. Every time he'd gotten close, she'd managed to pull away.

But tonight she'd given him a green light. The first. She'd opened up and let him in, and he'd be damned if he let her throw up that red light permanently. West had no doubt he was in for a bumpy trip in his pursuit of Kelsey, but as long as he got to the destination he was aiming for, he'd put up with a few stop-starts.

KELSEY TOOK a deep breath and got out of the car, lugging her briefcase over the console behind her. She'd been dreading this meeting since Friday night when West had left her breathless and confused with her door closed between them. And frustrated. God. He'd left her so sexually wound up that she'd resorted to taking care of things herself every night since. Three times and she still walked on the jagged edge of arousal.

She'd barely made it through the weekend without tearing her hair out. Or driving over to West's place to demand he finish what he started. The smoldering desire she'd lived with for years had turned into a blaze with only a kiss. Then again, her body knew what he could do when he set his mind to it, and surely he'd improved his skills over the last ten years. She shivered. Lord, just the thought of what he'd learned had her pulse skipping and her insides melting.

He'd had serious talent as a novice, and he hadn't been afraid to try something new or push for more all those years ago either, so he was bound to have gotten better. Another shiver skipped over her skin, pulling a wave of goose bumps behind it. Her stride faltered as the door to West's building opened and the man himself stepped out.

"Hey, I've been waiting for you." He came towards her, his hand outstretched. "Let me take that for you."

She let him take her bag more because she didn't have the brainpower to protest than anything else.

"Tough day?" he asked as he placed a hand on her lower back and guided her towards the door.

"What? Oh, no, not really. But it's been a full one." Kelsey wasn't about to tell him she hadn't slept well since their kiss. He already had enough power over her without giving him that piece of information.

"Have you eaten?" West reached out to open the door. "I can make you a snack if you're hungry."

"No. I'm good. I grabbed a burger for lunch." As soon as the words left her mouth she knew she was in trouble.

"A burger?" He pulled her to a stop. "Please tell me you are not referring to one of those things they serve at the Golden Arches."

Kelsey ducked her head. "Then I won't."

"Jeez, Kels, you can't live on that crap."

"I don't. I eat other stuff."

"Frozen diet meals don't count in the not-crap column either."

Damn. He knew her so well. "Fine. I promise to eat better if you promise to take my advice and hire a fulltime office manager." Kelsey wasn't above using her capitulation to get something she wanted. It didn't matter that it was something West needed desperately.

"Deal. When do you start?"

"I'll start by making a healthy chicken salad for dinner tonight."

"I'm talking about work."

"What?"

"I'm happy for you to continue seeing your regular clients out of here if that makes things easier." West steered her into the small windowless room he used as an office.

"Wait. What?" Had she missed something he said? She must have, because she was completely lost in this conversation.

"Sit. I'll get you a drink." He pushed her into the chair behind his desk and left the room before she could blink.

What the hell had just happened? Kelsey ran back over every word they'd spoken, and even though she thought she had a handle on it, the outcome didn't make any sense. West was talking as if she'd agreed to be his new office manager. It wasn't the first time he'd suggested it, but she'd never believed he meant it as a real possibility. He couldn't be serious. Could he?

She mulled over the idea while pulling files out of her briefcase. Spying a folder overflowing with invoices, Kelsey tried not to panic at the thought of all those numbers not being entered into the relevant spreadsheets she'd set up for West's business. With a sinking feeling, she began leafing through the paperwork on his desk. She'd just booted up his computer when he came back in.

"Here. This will go a long way to repairing the damage that processed burger is doing to your system." He placed a bright-green drink in front of her.

"What the hell is that?" Kelsey leaned over and took a sniff. "Banana?"

"Yep, with some extra nutrients thrown in."

Oh God. He was feeding her one of those super smoothie things his sister made. Kelsey scrunched up her nose as she took another sniff.

"Just drink it. It won't kill you." He flopped into the chair on the other side of his desk.

"But it's green."

"It's only kale and spinach. Nothing sinister, I promise."

Kelsey eyed the glass as she picked it up and brought it to her lips. She took a tentative sip and was surprised by the sweet banana flavor that burst across her tongue. Taking a bigger drink, she tried to determine what else he'd added to it.

"Good?" West watched her with a grin on his face.

"It's okay." Kelsey wasn't about to admit the damn thing tasted yummy. She took another drink before she put the glass down and opened the file that held West's tax documents. "Now if you'll pull up the spreadsheets for me, I'll get started."

"Ah, yeah, about that…"

She glanced up, eyebrows raised.

"I kinda, sorta haven't gotten to those." He lifted his chin in the direction of the overflowing folder.

"Dammit, West." This was going to take so much longer than she'd thought—hoped. With a sigh, she leaned back in the chair. "You promised me this year would be different."

"I know. And it would have been. But time got away from me, and today I got caught up in the kitchen."

Kelsey held up her hand. "I don't want to hear excuses. This is why you need an office manager."

"I know."

"Then hire one."

"I want you."

The words hung in the air between them. He'd said those exact words numerous times before when they'd talked about his need for a fulltime manager, but after Friday night's kiss, those three simple words took on a whole new meaning.

From head to toes, everything tightened, warmed and tingled, and a full-body shiver rolled over her. His eyes went dark, his gaze laser-like in its intensity, and Kelsey's breath hitched. She licked her lips, her tongue sticking on the dry surface. West's hands fisted on his thighs and her eyes were drawn to the bulge in his pants. He didn't hide from her, and if she was reading him right, he wanted her to know exactly what he wanted her for.

"West." His name was a plea on her lips, but Kelsey had no clue what she was asking for.

"Take the job, Kels." The words came through clenched teeth.

"I have a job. A business."

West sucked in a deep breath and let it out slowly. As she watched, his shoulders relaxed and his hands opened. "Yes, and we both know that things are going to get slow now that tax season is coming to an end."

"I still have clients," she argued.

He nodded. "And I'll bet you next year's profits that you can manage those as well as Weston's. With your hands tied behind your back."

Kelsey opened her mouth to argue further, but she couldn't come up with another excuse to refuse the job. Not without revealing her feelings, and she wasn't ready for West to know how deep those went. Besides, her business was about to shrink, and with it her income. Not that she was in any danger of going broke. Tax time might be exhaustingly busy, but it was also extremely lucrative. She closed her eyes and leaned her head back against the chair.

Leather creaked, but she kept her eyes shut, not wanting to see him just now for fear one look into those storm-cloud eyes would seal her fate. His feet brushed over the concrete floor as he moved around, and it only took a moment to work out he was walking around the desk towards her. She heard him crouch down beside her, felt the light brush of his hand over her denim covered knee.

"Kels. Look at me."

She swallowed, her constricted throat aching as the muscles worked. Slowly, she raised her eyelids and turned her head to meet his gaze.

"Give me a year. One year to make it work for both of us."

She wanted to say yes. God, did she. But there was more at stake than their perspective businesses. If she said yes, she'd be in West's presence every day. There'd be no hiding from her feelings and certainly no stopping them from growing deeper. Day in, day out, Kelsey would be faced with her biggest weakness.

Weston Mann.

3

———————

West held his breath. He could see Kelsey wavering. Could see she wanted to say yes, but something held her back, and he had a sinking feeling it was what lay unspoken between them. They'd never talked about what they'd done, and he couldn't decide whether he should bring it up now or let it lie. His gut told him opening up that topic might destroy any chance he had of building a future with her, and he wasn't prepared to risk that. Not yet. First, he needed to convince her to take the job so he could spend more time with her.

"C'mon. You and I both know you can do the work with your eyes closed. Plus, you already know the system inside out. It's yours after all." He hoped a little flattery would sway her.

She let out a harsh breath. "Fine. A year. But if at any time between now and then, I can't keep up with my existing clients, the deal's off."

Before she could change her mind, he thrust out his hand. "Deal." Kelsey put her hand in his and it took considerable control he didn't think he had not to pull her from the chair and into his lap.

"Don't think for one second me taking the job gets you out of inputting all those invoices," she said as she untangled her hand from his.

"Isn't that your job?"

"Yes. But not until next Monday. I'll need the rest of this week to get everything figured out if I'm going to run my business alongside yours. We don't want—or need—any glitches in the transition." She pushed the chair back and stood. "Have at it."

He shot to his feet. "Where are you going?"

Kelsey jerked back, one eyebrow arching almost to her hairline. "To the bathroom?"

"Oh. Right." West took a deep breath and moved out of her way. "I'll, um, get started on these then." He indicated the overflowing folder on his desk.

She gave him a smile that was more a grimace before edging past him and leaving the room. West shook his head as he dropped into his chair. He really needed to get a hold of himself. No one and nothing could rattle him like Kelsey. It had been that way since high school when he'd secretly lusted after her. Of course, he'd been a juvenile idiot back then. Proof being the way he'd handled the whole sleeping-together thing. He'd fucked it up royally and had thought any chance to be with her had disappeared the day she'd said I do to his friend.

And now, three years after Kels and Bry had parted ways, he couldn't hold back his desire or his need to be with her. He had a plan, he'd come up with it over the weekend, and she'd just said yes to the first stage. She'd given him a year, but West didn't think he'd need that long to get what he wanted. He'd seen the heat in her gaze —felt it in the bone-melting kiss they'd shared last Friday. He knew she wanted him and their attraction went both ways. But would she act on her feelings?

Jesus, he hoped so. Hoped with every fiber of his being. Not wanting to be in her bad books before they even got started, West flipped open the folder of invoices he'd neglected and brought up the spreadsheet Kelsey had made for him to enter his business expenses. He wasn't the smartest when it came to computers, but he prided himself on being a quick study. Unfortunately, the complicated charts that Kels had first given him had proven idiot proof. He'd been the biggest idiot in the bunch, so she'd put together something more his speed.

By the time Kelsey returned from the bathroom, West had punched in the numbers on four invoices and was working on the fifth. He tried not to be distracted when Kels sat on the other side of his desk. Tried not to watch her slender fingers tapping over the keys of her laptop. Or the way her reading glasses kept sliding down her nose. But it was hard when her perfume—something sweet smelling like one of the sugary desserts he made—floated around him, reminding him of her taste.

With a groan, he deleted the wrong figures. Again. That made three times he'd attempted to enter the same fucking number.

"Something wrong?"

West glanced up to find Kelsey leaning across the desk in an effort to see his screen. She wore a simple tee. Nothing fancy or revealing or sexy. But her lower arms were resting on the desktop, the upper section pressing into her sides and pushing her breasts together in a way that made the V-neck of her top gap open to reveal a cleavage of smooth, tanned skin. He swallowed. Hard.

He licked his lips and opened his mouth but only a garbled croak came out.

She raised her eyebrows. "You okay?"

Nodding, he spotted the smoothie he'd made her and reached for it. He took a mouthful to wet his parched mouth and throat. "Yep. I'm good."

A smile kicked up one corner of her lips. "I guess I know why you're always avoiding doing your books."

"Huh?" West took another sip of her drink before putting it down.

"Obviously, your creative brain can't handle numbers."

"Creative?"

"You don't consider yourself creative?" she asked as she picked up the glass and brought it to her mouth.

He shook his head. "Ah..." Jesus. She was going to put her mouth right where his had been. Why that should send a burst of lust through his system, he hadn't a clue, but that's exactly what it did. Blood rushed south to fill his groin, making his jeans tight, and he cursed the fact he'd had to go commando this morning because he'd forgotten to do his washing again. His cock pressed into the thick denim of his zipper and West shifted in his seat in the hope of giving himself a little bit of room. It didn't work.

Kelsey watched him closely over the top of her glasses and he stopped squirming instantly. The last thing he wanted was for her to figure out how worked up he was having her sitting across the desk from him. She'd retract her acceptance of the job and head out the door in a second if she thought he couldn't control himself around her. He picked up the invoice and turned back to the monitor to focus on the numbers in front of him and not the pain in his groin or the urge gnawing at his insides to throw her on his desk and take her hard and fast.

~

KELSEY COULDN'T BELIEVE she'd agreed to take the job as West's office manager. She had no one to blame but herself for giving in though. He'd looked at her with those stormy eyes and she'd folded quicker than a house of cards in a light tropical breeze. They'd been at his desk working for over an hour now. She'd been done in half that time but had worked on a to-do list for making the transition to working at Weston's while she waited for him to finish keying in his invoices.

It probably would have been more expedient to do them herself, except she didn't want West to think he could get away with pushing them off onto her again. He'd done it every year since she'd taken Weston's on as a client, and regardless of whether she minded or not, it didn't sit well with her knowing she'd given him special treatment because of their friendship. She would never allow any of her other clients to get away with it.

She sighed. But then West wasn't just any old client.

West slapped the last sheet on top of the pile, making her jump.

"Done." He flopped back in his chair as though he'd run a marathon.

She couldn't help it. She burst out laughing.

"Hey." He scowled at her.

"C'mon, it's not that bad." Kelsey reached over for the invoices, stood them up, and tapped them on the desk to straighten the pile. "Pass me a paperclip."

West opened his top drawer and rummaged around inside for a minute. When he slammed the drawer closed and opened the second, Kelsey smiled.

"Never mind. I've got one." She unzipped the side pocket on her briefcase, slipped her hand inside and came out with a handful of clips. "Here, throw the rest in your drawer."

"It's your drawer now."

Kelsey grinned. "Not until next week it's not."

West's forehead creased and she could tell he was contemplating something serious. Instead of asking him what as she normally would, she busied herself with setting out her paperwork for his tax return.

"Can you put your spreadsheets on this for me?" Kelsey pushed the memory stick she used for Weston's financial files towards him.

"Sure."

She waited for him to load the USB and pass it back. Once he did, she plugged it into her laptop and got to work.

"Anything else?"

Focused on her screen, she shook her head and continued to combine the information he'd given her with the year's spreadsheet. She was surprised to feel a release of tension in her shoulders a few minutes later and glanced up to discover West had left the office. The fact she noticed his departure on such a cellular level worried her. He was more than under her skin and always had been. And with her taking on a more permanent role in his business, she wondered how long it would be before she gave in to her desire and fell into bed with him.

The muffled sound of her phone chirping came from her briefcase. She was waiting to hear from Shaye, so she leaned over to retrieve it from her bag. Kelsey laughed out loud when she read the text.

OMFG! Get me out of here!

Kelsey hadn't even hit reply when the thing vibrated and chirped again.

GIRLS' NIGHT! Your place at 7!

Uh oh. For Shaye to want a girls' night on Monday, things obviously hadn't improved at work since last week. Kelsey quickly fired back a reply.

Things no better?

It was a while before her friend texted back, and Kelsey had started to worry. That didn't improve at all when Shaye finally replied.

Worse! Talk later.

"Shit."

"What's the matter? Am I in for a bigger tax bill than we projected? I know this last quarter's income went beyond expected." West put a plate of sliced fruit on the table in front of her.

"Ah, no." She held up her phone. "Shaye just texted me."

"Still problems with her boss?"

Kelsey sighed. Shaye had told everyone on Friday night that her boss had started making inappropriate comments and suggestions. She'd been hoping Zac would have some advice on how to handle it seeing how he was a lawyer. Unfortunately, he'd only repeated what Kelsey had already told her. She needed to go to HR and report the man. "See for yourself." She handed him her phone.

"Wow. She really needs to report him."

"She can't afford to lose her job."

"If she lost her job over that, she'd have grounds to sue the company." West handed her phone back. "Want me to throw together something for you guys to have for dinner?"

Kelsey knew he would in a heartbeat, but she didn't want to put him out or let him in to her life anymore today than she already had. "Nah, but thanks. We'll order pizza."

He shuddered and pulled a face, making Kelsey laugh.

"What?" he asked.

"There's nothing wrong with pizza."

"No, but I can send you home with a nice homemade lasagna to go with the alcohol you're both liable to consume while Shaye bitches about her boss."

Her mouth watered. She glanced at the time on her laptop. "You can make lasagna in an hour?" Kelsey couldn't believe how tempted she was.

"Sure. It'll only take me thirty minutes tops, and all you'll have to do when you get home is stick it in the oven on one-eighty for about the same."

Damn, she was tempted. So tempted. West made the best lasagna Kelsey had ever tasted, and it had been weeks since she'd had some. "Are you sure?" she asked.

"Consider it done." He walked around behind his desk and dropped into his chair. "Now what can I do to help get this tax return done?"

"Nothing. I just need to finish generating the yearly reports off the spreadsheets and then enter the info in your return and we're done for another year." Kelsey smiled.

"Really? Are you sure there's nothing I can do?"

"Positive."

"Okay." He pressed his hands on his desk as he stood up. "Then I'll go get that lasagna started."

"Okay, but if it's too much trouble or you have something else to do, we can just have pizza." Kelsey didn't really want pizza now that West had her thinking about his lasagna, but she didn't want to put him out either.

"No trouble. I have to whip up a batch of curry anyway." He started around his desk. "If I'm not back before you finish, come find me."

Once West left, Kelsey went back to work. It didn't take her long to have everything ready to file with the tax department, and because she did that electronically, she just had to give the forms one final read through and she'd be done. He was lucky. The business may have generated higher-than-expected earnings last quarter, but the staff, equipment and supplies he'd added in recent months offset that enough that he didn't owe that much more tax than they'd calculated at the beginning of the financial year.

West still hadn't come back by the time she was finished, so she saved her files and switched off her laptop. She'd print out his copies later. Of course, now that she'd be working for him, it would be her responsibility to file them away, so it wouldn't make a difference if he didn't have them until next week. He certainly wouldn't bother putting them away himself. She smiled when she thought about his aversion to office work. Probably a good thing she liked it seeing how she'd taken on the job to get Weston's organized.

With everything packed up, Kelsey walked around West's desk and closed all open programs on his computer before shutting it down. She thought about going through his office supplies and writing a list of what was needed but her phone buzzed, signaling another text. Glancing over, she saw it was from Shaye and reached over to pick it up. The message made her stomach tighten.

Do you still have a spare key hidden in the frog in your backyard?

Her spare key? Another message popped up.

I'm at your place now.

Kelsey glanced at the time with shock, but she quickly recovered to send Shaye a reply. *Yes. What happened?*

Quit!

What the fuck? Shaye had quit her job? Thumbs flying over the screen, Kelsey sent another text. *What did that asshole do?*

I'll explain when you get here. I'm in. :-)

Kelsey stared at her phone for long seconds before she snapped out of it and gathered her things together. She needed to head home now. Shaye wouldn't have quit over something minor. She'd been putting up with her boss's inappropriate behavior for months, so to Kelsey's mind that meant the man had crossed the line from inappropriate to downright indecent.

Briefcase in one hand, keys and phone in the other, Kelsey made her way out of the office and across the warehouse towards the kitchen that took up the back half of the building. She found West standing in front of the stove, stirring something that smelled absolutely divine. Her tummy rumbled.

"I have to go."

He turned her way. "What? Why?"

"Shaye just sent a text saying she quit."

"Quit? Her job? Why?"

She shrugged. "I don't know, but she's already at my place so I want to get there right away."

"Of course."

"I'm sorry about dinner. We'll just order pizza after all."

"Nonsense. I'll put this together and drop it off later."

"I can't ask you to do that," she argued.

"You didn't ask. Your place is on my way home, and all I have to do is wait for this sauce to thicken then put it together. No trouble at all."

"Are you sure?" She hated to put him out, but it did smell delicious and she really didn't have time to argue.

"Definitely." He took the saucepan off the heat but continued to stir. "Just about done now, but you go. I'll bring it by in an hour or so."

"Okay. Thanks." She turned to leave but only got a few steps when he called out.

"Kelsey. Ring me if you or Shaye need anything."

She looked over her shoulder and smiled. He was always ready to help her with anything. A sharp pang of longing stabbed her. West made her want things she shouldn't. Screwing up her marriage with Bry had left a fear she just couldn't shake. If she and West took their friendship farther—if they crossed that line again—she stood to lose far more than just her heart. Her split with Bry hadn't damaged any of the close friendships in their group, but if anyone found out about her and West's history—if they found out she'd loved him all along, they'd never forgive her.

Especially Bry.

4

West re-read the text message he'd just received.

Give job Shaye.

He thought he understood, but he hoped like hell he was wrong. Earlier, when he'd dropped the lasagna at Kelsey's, she'd been well on her way to being drunk. And from the look of Shaye, she'd barely gotten started. He hovered his thumb over the screen while he debated whether or not to reply.

"What are you doing?" Coop asked as he sat on the couch beside him, a fresh beer in his hand.

Without taking his eyes off the phone, West said, "Trying to decide if I should go over to Kelsey's and remove all the alcohol or ignore her."

"What the fuck is going on with you two?" Zac growled from the other side of the room.

West glanced up at his best friend. "Nothing. Shaye's over there. They're getting drunk because Shaye quit her job today." West looked back down and hit reply just as another text came in.

Wasted! :)

He laughed as he fired back a response. *Shouldn't have had that second glass. ;)*

Lifting his head, West met his best friend's narrowed gaze once more. "I finally convinced Kels to take the job today." Zac and Coop both knew what he was talking about. Hell, their whole group would know, he'd been talking about trying to get Kels to work for him for months.

"She agreed?" Coop shook his head. "Never thought I'd hear that."

"Tell me you haven't touched her," Zac demanded.

Coop shot forward in his seat as beer sprayed out his mouth and rolled down his chin. "What?" he choked out while wiping his jaw with the back of his hand.

Zac stared West down, but West held his gaze and didn't answer either way.

"You and Kelsey?" Coop's words held curiosity, not censure.

"West."

"What, Zac? What do you want me to say? Of course I've touched her. She's my friend."

"That's not what I'm talking about, and you know it."

West scrubbed a hand down his face and blew out a breath. He could lie or he could hedge or he could just tell his two best friends the truth. His phone vibrated in his hand and he glanced down.

Second bottle did it.

He couldn't hold back his laughter, which of course only got him another dirty look from Zac.

"What's she saying?" Coop asked.

"That she's wasted."

"So she's had two glasses then," Coop said with a grin, and Zac couldn't help but laugh even if he tried to cover it by coughing. Everyone knew how much of a lightweight Kels was.

West was relieved to see Zac loosen up on the whole Kelsey thing for a second. Lord knows he was going to blow a gasket when West came clean about his intentions.

"When did Shaye quit?" Coop asked.

"This afternoon. Don't know the details, but I did see a couple of messages she sent Kels this afternoon that hinted at things being worse at work." On Friday night, he'd wanted to find Shaye's boss and slam the man's head through a wall when she'd told them what had been going on, but after today, West thought putting the guy's head through a wall might not be enough.

"Anyone know where we can find the guy?" Coop's words were laced with a steel edge that had West and Zac staring in his direction. "What?"

West lifted one brow. "Shaye?"

Coop relaxed back against the couch and brought his beer to his mouth. He took his time taking a sip before answering. "Problem?"

West looked at Zac who was shaking his head, a scowl on his face. Turning back to Coop he said, "Nope. Not from me. Just surprised."

"Been thinking on it for a while. Trying to gage whether it's worth pursuing or not. But after the conversation Friday night, and my gut reaction to it, I've figured out I'd be stupid not to." Coop pulled his phone from his pocket. "Let's see if I can get some drunk texts too."

West watched his friends. Coop appeared relaxed, but Zac's body held a tautness that told him revealing anything about his intentions regarding Kelsey might cause some friction that West wasn't interested in dealing with right now. Coop's unexpected revelation about his feelings for Shaye should take some of the sting out of his own admission, but with Zac's next words, West knew he'd have to keep his mouth shut unless he wanted a fight with one of his best friends.

"What is it with you guys wanting to fuck with the group?" Zac shook his head, his forehead wrinkled. "It wasn't bad enough when things went south with Bry and Kelsey?"

"Bad?" Coop lifted his gaze from his phone to look at his twin. "What the hell are you talking about? Those two should never have gotten married in the first place, and you know it. Their friendship is just as strong now as it was when they were sleeping together, Zac."

"Coop's right," West added in a calm voice despite the less-than-calm emotions churning his insides at the thought of Kels and Bry together. "There wasn't any drama when they split, which says a lot about their marriage."

Zac frowned.

"Theirs was never really an overly passionate relationship," West said as razor-sharp jealousy sliced at his insides and threatened to spew from his chest on a growl.

"And don't forget Kelsey moved out before anyone knew about the split. Shit, I don't remember them ever having a fight," Coop added.

West had known. He'd known because he'd helped her move some of her things. Of course, he hadn't said a word to anyone. Kels had wanted it kept quiet until after she'd filed the divorce papers and, as was West's usual MO when it came to Kelsey, he'd done whatever she asked.

West's phone buzzed. *I don't feel so good.* "Uh oh, Kels isn't going to last much longer."

Coop's phone went off and he burst out laughing when he read the text.

"What?" Zac asked as he got out of his chair and headed towards his brother. "Show me."

"You sure you want to see what we're saying, little brother?" Coop teased.

"Two minutes, for fuck's sake."

"Yeah, but those two minutes put you a whole day behind me." Coop grinned. The long-standing taunt got the usual reaction from Zac.

"Give me the phone." Zac lunged at Coop and the two of them wrestled on the couch until they rolled to the floor at West's feet.

Zac finally yanked the phone from Coop's hand. He scanned the screen quickly. "Jesus. Are you for real?"

West leaned over and grabbed Zac's wrist to keep the phone still so he could see the exchange between Coop and Shaye.

So my buddy is getting some text messages from your drunk friend. Wanna play too?

I'll play with you anytime, stud. ;-)

"Holy shit!" West said.

Coop grinned. "Yeah. I think I'm going to see if she needs a ride home."

Zac tossed the phone at his brother as he climbed to his feet. "You two are sick."

"What the fuck is up your ass, Zac?" Coop sat up.

"Nothing." Zac bent to retrieve his keys and phone from the floor beside his chair. "I'm outta here. Catch you dickheads later."

Before either of them spoke, Zac was gone. West turned to Coop. "What's going on with him?"

"Hell if I know. I was planning to ask you. He's been weird for a while now. Ever since he helped Cassie out with that party a few months back." Coop shook his head. "And before you ask, neither Cassie nor Dan can remember anything happening that night. I already asked. Maybe something's going on at work?"

"Hmm..." West had an inkling of what might be going on with Zac, but he didn't want to bring it up with Coop yet. He'd have a chat with Dan next time he saw him and double-check his suspicions. "Enough about grumpy. Are you really going to play with Shaye?"

"Don't see why I shouldn't, in spite of Zac's objection."

"You're not worried about what it'll do to the group dynamic if things go south?" West asked. It was something he'd considered when contemplating him and Kelsey. Although at this point he'd decided he didn't care how the group was affected.

"If I went into every relationship thinking it was going to end, it wouldn't be worth bothering, would it?" Coop shrugged. "Besides, I'm not about to let something that could be great pass me by just because it might upset some of my friends."

"Guess you have to weigh up whether the possible outcome is worth the risk."

"Oh, she's worth it." Coop grinned as he began poking at his phone again. "Now if you'll excuse me, I'm going to offer my services as a designated driver."

"Is that the only service you're offering?"

Coop laughed. "I'm game for anything with Shaye."

West stood up as Coop's phone beeped. "She say yes?"

"Sure did."

"Do me a favor? Check on Kels when you pick Shaye up. Make sure she isn't going to be sleeping in her own vomit."

"What do I look like? Your slave boy?" Coop pulled his keys from his pocket. "If you're that worried, head over there and check on her yourself."

West frowned. He wasn't sure going around to Kelsey's was a good idea, but he wanted to make sure she was all right. If she wasn't lying about the two bottles of wine, she was going to be one sorry woman come morning unless she flushed her system with water now. A couple of aspirin wouldn't hurt either. "Just send me a text telling me how trashed she is."

"Fine. But avoiding her isn't going to fix your problem," Coop said as he pulled West's front door open.

"What's that supposed to mean?"

"Man up, West."

"Hey!"

"Don't give me that shit. You might never mention it and think you've managed to keep your feelings for Kelsey secret, but you're forgetting who you're talking to. I know you. I remember the crush you had on her back in school."

"That was then." West tried to brush it off.

"Yeah, and this is now, and she's no longer trapped in a passionless marriage with one of our closest friends." Coop clapped his hand on West's shoulder. "Don't let what Zac says, or what anyone else, especially Bry, might think stop you from going after what you really want. She's worth the risk."

With those parting words, Coop left him standing in his foyer, wondering if his friend was the only one who'd seen through his facade to the deeper emotions for Kelsey lurking beneath. Zac had certainly picked up on it, but then out of the two Moreland twins, West and Zac were closest, so that was to be expected. Sighing, he reached over and flipped the deadlock before heading back into the lounge room and picking up his empty bottle. He'd dumped it in the trash and put away the leftover food before his phone buzzed with the text he was waiting for.

She's already driving the porcelain bus. Get your ass round here now. We'll wait until you're here before we leave.

"Shit!"

It didn't matter how much he thought he should stay away from Kels right now, there was no way he was going to let her suffer alone. Figuring he'd be spending the night at her house, West threw a change of clothes and his toiletries in a bag before racing out the door.

KELSEY'S STOMACH HURT. Her head hurt. Even her butt hurt where she was sitting on the cold tile floor. And her mouth tasted like shit. Not that she knew what shit actually tasted like, but she thought it was probably close to the ghastly flavor coating her tongue and teeth.

"Oh God," she moaned as another wave of nausea squeezed her belly, only she'd already emptied out her stomach. That included the lining. Or at least that's what it felt like.

"Here, put this on your forehead."

West.

"Go away." Kelsey wasn't sure if he understood her. Her tongue kept sticking to the roof of her mouth and her lips were so dry it felt as though they'd shrunk three sizes. *Do lips come in sizes?*

"I'm sure you'd like that, but it's not happening."

Her head spun when West scooped her up off the bathroom floor and carried her from the room. "Where...?" She couldn't manage the rest of the sentence. Her brain was too busy impersonating a merry-go-round on speed.

"Easy, there."

"Dizzy."

"Keep still and it won't be so bad."

He placed her on her bed. She knew it was her bed because she could smell the scented candle she had sitting on her bedside table and the softness of her mattress cradled her hurting body. "Damn Shaye."

West chuckled. "Yeah, well, you should have known better than to try to keep up with her."

"She needed me."

"I don't think she needed you to make yourself sick." He slid his hand under head and lifted. "Here. Try to get some of this down."

Cool glass was pressed against her lips. She opened her mouth and took a few sips, but her coordination wasn't the best and some of the water spilled over her lips and down her chin.

"Slow down." West pulled the drink away and eased her back against the pillow.

His warmth disappeared and Kelsey reached out blindly. "Don't go."

"I'm not going anywhere." He wiped her face. "Do you want anything else?"

"You."

"I'm right here."

"'Kay." His fingers brushed the hair from her face and she moved into his touch. "Feels nice," she murmured.

"Mmm."

"Don't stop." Kelsey snuggled into the bedding. "Don't ever stop."

Her stomach continued to churn and her head was all floaty, but the soothing rhythm of West's gentle strokes across her temple soon had her drifting in and out of sleep.

Kelsey wasn't sure what disturbed her, but she knew exactly what it was that catapulted her out of sleep. There was someone in bed with her. And not just *any* someone. West. She'd know his scent anywhere, and it was definitely him she was currently wrapped around like white on rice. Oh my God. What had she done? She remembered coming home to find Shaye already into the first bottle of wine. Then they'd opened a second...

Damn. She couldn't remember beyond that. Gingerly, Kelsey tried to untangle her legs from his, but she'd managed to get herself well and truly pinned by one of his legs. They were lying on their sides, her face smashed up against his chest. At least he had a shirt on. And if she was right, they both had pants on too.

"Stop freaking out and go back to sleep."

Kelsey jolted at the sound of West's voice.

"Unless you need to go to the bathroom or want a drink stay right where you are."

"But—"

"Not listening." He tightened his arms around her. "Go back to sleep."

She lay there with thoughts bouncing around her head. When had West come over? And when the hell had they climbed into bed together? Why had they gotten into bed if they still had their clothes on? Kelsey could only think of one reason to crawl into bed with West, and it wasn't to sleep.

"Kels, quit worrying this to death. You were drunk. I held your hair out of the toilet and made sure you got to bed, at which point you ask me to stay. I did. End of story. Now go back to sleep. We have to be up in a few hours."

"I can't remember what happened after Shaye opened the second bottle." Kelsey hated admitting her lack of memory, but she knew West would be honest with her regardless of how bad the truth was, and she really, *really* needed to know what had led up to him being in her bed.

"Nothing happened, if that's what you're worrying about." West slid his hand up her spine and cupped her nape, moving his thumb and fingers in circles on either side of her neck. "I'd never take advantage of you like that."

She sighed. Of course he wouldn't. Worst luck. If he did, she wouldn't have to worry about making the decision to go there again. It wouldn't be her fault.

West chuckled. "You don't really want me to make it that easy for you, do you?"

"W-what?"

"I know you. You're thinking if I took advantage of your drunken state to get you naked underneath me you wouldn't have to take responsibility for your actions." He tangled his fingers in her hair, massaged the back of her head with hypnotic pressure. "When you find yourself under me again—and make no mistake, you will sometime soon—you'll know exactly what you're doing. And you'll remember every damn second of it."

"Oh."

5

West leaned against the counter and rubbed his eyes with his thumb and index finger. They were dry and gritty from too little sleep. It was barely ten a.m. and he was ready to crawl back into bed, and for once he wasn't thinking about Kelsey being under him in it. He'd had her there last night. All soft and malleable and smelling like a brewery. He smiled. If she ever found out some of the things she'd said in her drunken stupor, she'd die of embarrassment.

Good thing he'd been the only one around and had no intention of telling anyone what her loose tongue had revealed. She'd mumbled plenty while she'd drifted off to sleep. From how good it felt when he touched her to how good he smelled. How much she'd missed him. Which seemed weird when they'd never lost touch. And, of course, the big one. She loved him. West didn't think he could hold her to that confession, but he was going to take the thrill that had coursed through him at her words and run with it.

He'd give anything to hear those words pass her sexy lips while she was stone-cold sober. He figured he'd be waiting a while though. The phone at his hip rang and he unhooked it from his belt to see who was calling now. It had been a morning of one thing after another. That was why he was working in his back-up kitchen at Are You Game? He wanted to avoid people at all costs this morning. Didn't help that he'd rather not have come to work at all, especially when he'd had to crawl out of bed where the woman of his dreams was sleeping beside him.

Seeing Kelsey's face and name illuminated on his screen sent a flurry of emotions through him. A little excitement, a bit of relief and a good dose of anxiety tangled together to have him staring at the device through five rings. Fear of her hanging up or the call switching over to voicemail had him sliding his finger across the screen to answer.

"Hey."

"You lied," Kelsey groaned.

West chuckled. She sounded horrible, and if he didn't know it was self-inflicted misery, he'd be more sympathetic. "About?"

"I'm not feeling any better than when you left this morning."

West could hear the whine in her voice and imagined her lying on her bed with one arm thrown up over her face. "Take some more aspirin."

"Did."

"When?"

"Now."

He laughed. "Give them a chance to work."

"I feel like my head is going to explode."

"I promise you it's not."

"Cross your heart?"

"Yes. Why don't you go back to bed for a few more hours?"

"Can't. Gotta work."

"Kelsey, you work for yourself, you can take a few hours off and catch up later."

"I'll be dead then."

He smiled at her melodramatic performance. It wasn't like her to complain. Then again, it wasn't like her to tie one on either. "You better not be dead. You have to be in the office at nine a.m. sharp Monday morning."

"About that…"

West could hear the words before she said them. "Don't you dare go back on our deal. You promised me a year."

"That was before."

"Before what?" He knew what she was thinking. They'd wound up in bed together, and while the night had been innocent, the temptation had been there. If he wasn't such a stand-up guy, he'd have made a move on her. They both knew it.

"*West.*" His name came down the line on a sigh.

He wasn't about to let her back out. "Here's the thing. There's something between us. There always has been, and we need to work that out. But right now, I need you in my office more, so you stick to your end of the deal and I promise I won't push you on a personal front." Jesus. What the hell was he saying?

"God. My head hurts too much to think straight," she murmured.

"Then don't think about any of it for now. Go back to bed and I'll be over later to check on you and bring some food." Maybe she'd forget his stupid words by then and he could continue with his original plan of slowly seducing her into his bed. His life.

"You can't keep feeding me."

"Why not?"

"Because you can't, that's why." Her voice rose slightly. "Oh, God," she moaned, and he could picture her holding her head.

"Go back to bed. We'll talk about it later."

She was silent for so long, West thought she'd hung up. He even pulled the phone away from his ear to check.

Bringing it back to his head, he said, "Kels? You still there?"

"Yeah, I'm here." Her heavy sigh filled his ear. "I don't know if I can do this."

He wanted to reassure her, but she wasn't the only one worried about what would happen, and he couldn't find the words to appease either of them right now. All he knew was he couldn't walk away. Not again. "Get some more sleep. I'll see you later."

"Okay," she whispered, a second before the line went dead.

West dropped his arm by his side and hung his head until his chin hit his chest. He had no idea what they were doing. He'd had a plan, but in light of last night he didn't think it would work as it stood, and he certainly hadn't factored in Kelsey's drunken ramblings. After those revelations, there was no way he was giving up. If anything, he wanted to race towards the finish line. Suppressing the urge to rush was going to be hard, but for the sake of all that was at risk, he'd do it.

He slipped his phone back onto his belt and pushed off the counter. It wouldn't matter how much he stressed over the situation. They'd just have to find their way one step at a time.

KELSEY SAT on the edge of her seat. Literally and figuratively. She'd been waiting hours for West to show up. During the endless afternoon, she'd gone over her speech a million times. She'd prepared it as well as she had any of the debates she'd participated in back in high school. There wasn't a box of trophies in her parents' attic for nothing. All she had to do was stick to the argument. Except she had a sneaky suspicion that with West right in front of her, every solid, reasonable justification of why they shouldn't get together would be swept aside as nothing more than flimsy excuses.

A rush of air left her lungs as she slumped back on the couch. She closed her eyes and hoped for strength. But she had the horrible feeling that nothing short of a miracle could save her from her own heart. That traitorous organ had been firmly on West's side for as long as she could remember. Add in the one night she'd spent in his arms and Kelsey didn't think she stood a chance of stopping this thing between them developing further.

The sound of a car pulling up outside had her eyes springing open and her body bolting upright. On her feet, she twisted her fingers together and toyed with the idea of pretending she wasn't home. Only her car was in the driveway where she'd left it and West knew she'd never risk getting behind the wheel if there was even a slight chance she still had alcohol in her system. Taking a deep breath, Kelsey screwed up her courage and headed for the front door.

After waiting what felt like an eternity for West to ring the bell, Kelsey moved to the side of the door to peek through the front window. Cracking the blind a tiny bit, she peered out into the fading light of day and discovered no car on the street or in her driveway other than her own. Laughter bubbled up her throat, the slight hysterical edge only making her laugh more. She was such an idiot.

Light flooded the road right before West's familiar four-wheel drive appeared and turned into her driveway to park beside her small hatchback. The laughter of moments ago turned into a choked sob and Kelsey whipped her hand away from the blind and took several steps back, only stopping when she collided with the wall behind her.

"Oh God."

She brought her hand up to cover her mouth, her fingers trembling. Fear? Anticipation? Kelsey couldn't decide what set her nerves to shaking, but she couldn't deny that West did one thing that had been missing for years. He made her feel deeply, made her yearn for something she thought she'd found only to discover it was a poor substitute for the real thing.

"Oh my God."

Was that it? Was what she felt for West the real thing?

Kelsey had known all along she didn't love Bry the way she loved West, but she'd never thought too much about the differences in the two sentiments, figuring her mind had blown her youthful love out of proportion, and what she had with Bry was the grownup version. Yes, Bry was her friend, one of her best friends still, and she loved him. But with hindsight, she knew she hadn't been *in love* with him. She hadn't wanted him with the same need she'd always wanted West. A bone-deep ache that had never gone away.

Guilt filled her chest, making it hard to draw a breath. She'd let her wounded heart be soothed by the easy love Bry had offered in those first few years after West's rejection. She'd accepted Bry's proposal of marriage because she'd wanted a home, a family, but not with the enthusiasm of a blushing bride. It had just seemed like the logical next step in their relationship.

God. She'd cheated both herself and Bry of so much. She should never have agreed to get married. Should never have waited—hoped —so long for their love to grow—deepen. Kelsey leaned against the wall and closed her eyes as a lump of regret lodged in her throat and tears stung her eyes.

"Kels? You okay?"

Her eyes snapped open as a scream ripped from her chest.

"Hey, hey, it's just me." West stepped forward, letting the front door close behind him.

"H-how'd you get in?" she asked to the accompaniment of her pounding heart.

West held up a key. "You gave it to me for emergencies, remember?"

"Oh, right." She'd forgotten all about giving him a spare.

"Are you still feeling sick? You don't look too good." He cupped her shoulders and bent so they were eye to eye. "Why aren't you lying down?"

She couldn't tell him what had put the sick look on her face. Not without revealing she'd carried—still held—a torch for him all these years. "Just a little lightheaded. Must have got up too quickly or something." Kelsey forced a smile and moved out of his grip.

He eyed her warily for a moment longer before bending to grab the bag at his feet she hadn't noticed until now. "Hungry?"

"Um, sure." Kelsey turned and led the way to her kitchen. She could feel West's eyes on her with each step she took, and she tried to keep her steps smooth and even but feared he could tell she was ready to shoot through the roof at the slightest provocation.

When they reached the kitchen, Kelsey had no idea what to do or say, but obviously West didn't have that problem. He went straight to the island counter where he proceeded to remove food from the bag he'd brought in.

"Thought I'd put together a stir-fry," he said.

He appeared at home in her house. Without pause, he knew

where the pans were kept, where to find the utensils necessary to put their meal together, and Kelsey wondered when it was that he'd become so familiar with her home. "Do you need help?"

"No. I've got it." He glanced up but continued to dice an onion at a thousand miles an hour without missing a beat. "Why don't you go sit down? Watch some TV?"

She'd love nothing more than to leave the room. To hide somewhere in the house away from all the conflicting emotions West stirred just by being West, but she knew she wouldn't. As much as she wanted to avoid him—to stick her head in the sand and pretend there wasn't a big fat white elephant in the room—she wanted to be near him more.

With a sigh, Kelsey pulled out a stool at her small corner table and sat. "I'm good here. Are you sure you don't want a hand?"

"Nah, almost done." West grinned at her with that knee-wobbling smile that never failed to send her into a restless, flustered state. Oblivious to her reactions to him, he skillfully prepared their dinner.

Tense beyond tolerable, Kelsey tried to think of something to talk about that would relieve the strain. Something that wouldn't lead to awkward questions. "How was work?"

He looked up with a frown and shrugged. "The usual."

"Oh. Right. Good." She couldn't keep eye contact. Not with all those questions she didn't want to answer, or even hear, lurking in his piercing gray gaze.

"Kels."

She reluctantly met his gaze once more, but there must have been something in hers—some desperate plea in her expression—because he shook his head and turned to the stove where he lit the burner under the pan.

Kelsey leaned one elbow on the table and propped her chin in her hand while she watched West move around. For as long as she'd known him, he'd loved to cook. One of the few boys in their year to take cooking in high school, it had been a part of him from the beginning. And now, having a front row seat to a grownup West using his culinary skills, she had to admit it was totally hot. And she wasn't referring to the stove.

He moved with fluid grace and a confidence that spoke volumes. She'd never felt that confident about anything. Not even her job gave her that level of self-belief and she was a damn good accountant. It just wasn't enough. What would it be like to feel complete satisfaction in anything? Kelsey had never known that feeling. No, that was a lie. Once. Once she'd felt the glow of contentment so enormous she'd floated on a cloud for weeks. Until it had all come crashing down in the face of West's lack of interest.

"Hey." West clicked his fingers in front of her. "You still with me?"

"Sorry. What?" She blinked and brought her focus back to the man before her.

"I asked if you wanted to eat in here or out in the living room."

Kelsey stood up. "The living room will be more comfortable." It would also offer a distraction in the form of her TV.

"Here." He held out two plates filled with a yummy-smelling noodle stir-fry. "You take these and I'll grab drinks and cutlery."

She took their meal and headed towards the front of the house. She'd bought an older place when her divorce was final with the hope of doing it up. But so far, in the not quite two years she'd lived here, she'd done nothing more than line the cupboards with paper.

Putting their plates on her garage-sale coffee table, she sat on her worn secondhand couch and questioned why she was living with hand-me-down furniture when she could afford to purchase new. The only new things in the house were the TV and her bed. Everything else had been picked up cheap or given to her.

"Water good?" West asked as he put two glasses on the table in front of her. He held out a fork. "Dig in before it gets cold."

Kelsey stared at the scratched and scarred fork. Oh my God. Even the cutlery was secondhand. She raised her gaze to find West watching her with one eyebrow arched in question.

"Everything is old," she murmured.

Wrinkles creased his forehead as he sat beside her still holding the fork out to her. "Huh?"

"All my stuff. It's old and used and I have no idea why."

"*Okay.*"

"Don't you see?"

He shook his head. "No, I don't understand what you're talking about."

And then it dawned on her. She'd walked away from Bry with nothing. She let him keep their house, their furnishings, even her car. Sure, he'd paid her half the value of everything they owned in the divorce settlement, but before that she'd left with her clothes and half the money in their savings account. Why would she do that? It didn't make any sense. She'd always had secondhand belongings growing up and she'd vowed never to settle for second best again once she moved out of her childhood home.

Her gaze travelled around the room. Jesus. Even the blinds were used. She'd picked them up at the same garage sale as the coffee table, thinking they'd do for a few weeks until she bought new ones, only she still hadn't replaced them.

"Kels?" West put his hand on her knee, drawing her attention back to him.

Knowledge slammed into her like a punch to the stomach. She'd not only settled for second best when it came to her possessions. She'd settled for the love she felt for Bry instead of putting her heart on the line and going after the man she'd really wanted all those years ago.

6

West leaned back and extended his legs out in front of him. He laced his fingers together and rested them on his stomach as he settled his gaze on the TV. He'd wanted to talk to Kelsey. Wanted to get things out in the open, but he knew that would probably cause distress. For the moment, he was enjoying sitting together, relaxing while some sitcom played out on the screen before them.

The meal he'd cooked was gone, and he was pretty sure Kels was dozing off beside him. Another reason not to bring up the topic neither of them seemed to want to deal with. He hoped she drifted off to sleep so he could sit beside her for a few hours without the usual turmoil. No pressure. Lately, every time they saw each other the tension between them was so thick you could cut the air with a knife. But if she were asleep, those barriers she always erected when he was around would be down and he could drop his guard too. Not worry about every little move he made or word he said.

He yawned and did something he hadn't done since he was a teenager. Stretching his arms over his head, he rolled his shoulders before he brought his arms down to lie along the back of the couch. West grinned when Kelsey didn't flinch. If he was in luck, she was already on her way to the land of nods and wouldn't even notice his juvenile move.

A few minutes later, a soft snoring came from beside him and he leaned forward to get a look at her face. Sure enough, she'd fallen asleep. She was probably still feeling the draining effects of last night's binge. He always slept like the dead for the next few days after getting rolling drunk, and Kelsey's body wasn't used to consuming large amounts of alcohol so she was liable to feel it for a long time yet.

West thought about moving her to bed where she'd be more comfortable, but he figured she'd wake up and send him home, and he wasn't ready to leave yet. Wrapping his arm around her shoulders, he nudged her closer against his side and was pleased when not only didn't she protest the move, but she snuggled in. She turned towards him and nestled her head into the crook of his neck, splayed her hand over his chest.

You couldn't have removed the grin from his face with a crowbar. He continued to watch TV, but if someone asked him what was on he couldn't tell them. The woman beside him held his complete attention and he gave in to the urge to look at her. Her features were so delicate—high sculpted cheekbones, long, feathery lashes, her slender nose drawing down to an up-turned tip. And her lips… They were plump, but not that bee-stung look some women were into these days. No, Kelsey's were just right as far as West was concerned. He'd love to lean over and lay his mouth on hers, but he wasn't stupid and really didn't want her to send him packing just yet.

He ignored the TV and continued to stare at Kels. He'd been shocked when she'd cut off her long hair a few years back, but he understood it was a cleansing of sorts for her. She'd left her husband and was starting a new life, so it had seemed only fitting she should have a new look. And West had to admit he loved the shorter length. There was still plenty of hair to get his fingers tangled in, and the way it floated around her face giving her a just-out-of-bed look always managed to get his engine revving.

Not that he was ever idle when Kelsey was around. He'd spent years living with the low buzz of arousal where she was concerned. Amazing how she could get him worked up without trying, and it took concentrated effort by other women to even pique his interest, never mind get him off. He hadn't been a monk or anything like that. He was a healthy guy after all, but he hadn't been one to indulge in one-night stands.

His longest relationship had lasted a year. But he usually found himself losing interest long before that, and if he were honest, he'd have to admit the woman currently lying in his arms was the reason. Even when she'd been off-limits he'd held out a tiny bit of hope that he'd have her one day in the future. And didn't that make him a prick of a friend.

He scrubbed his free hand over his face. All this self-examination was doing his head in. Closing his eyes, he concentrated on the feel of Kelsey against him and the steady rush of her breath warming his skin through his shirt as she slept in his arms.

WEST WOKE with a pain in his neck and an elbow in his ribs. The neck ache was due to his head flopping forward in his sleep and the elbow belonged to the woman currently cursing under her breath and trying to crawl off him.

Kelsey.

He sucked in a jagged breath when her knee came dangerously close to his goods.

"Kels," he warned.

"Shit." West cracked one eye to see her glaring at him. "Don't do that!"

"Don't do what?" he grumbled. "I'm not the one inflicting grievous bodily harm."

"What?"

He glanced down at his groin where her knee was still firmly wedged between his thighs only centimeters from his balls.

"Oh my God." She planted her hands, fingers splayed, on his chest and pushed back. "Sorry. I didn't mean..."

Her words ground to a stop when she noticed things weren't exactly quiet down there. His usual morning woody was helped along by the fact she'd been plastered against him in all her curvaceous glory not five minutes ago. And while his jeans weren't skin tight, they certainly didn't offer enough room to hide eight inches of hard flesh from view.

"I...um..."

West kept his eyes on her face, so when she stammered over her stuttered breath and licked her lips, he all but burst from the zipper in his pants. "Kels." He wasn't sure what he was saying other than her name. Need rocketed through him, and if she didn't take her delectable ass off his lap in the next five seconds he wouldn't be responsible for where she ended up. Or down. He'd like her down. On her back, legs wide, waiting for him to plunge deep.

Kelsey's gaze slowly travelled up his torso until she met his eyes with ones swimming in emotion. West could see the struggle, knew his own gaze reflected the same desperate war of advance or retreat. In the end, it was need that won out.

He wasn't sure which one of them moved first. It didn't matter. Their lips fused in a kiss so hot, so wet his mind switched off and his body took over. Every nerve sparked with awareness until he felt like a livewire in urgent need of discharging latent energy. She slid her hands up his chest and scrunched her fingers in the fabric of his T-shirt as they took the kiss deeper.

She opened for him. Let him tease and take at his will. Her surrender fired his blood, filled his already hard cock with pounding heat. He shoved his hands into her hair and pinned her head in place so he could devour her mouth more. God, he wanted so much more. The whimper that slipped up her throat was sucked down his, and West knew if they didn't stop now, they wouldn't. And as much as he wanted to overwhelm her with desire to get what he wanted he couldn't.

Pulling his mouth from hers, he moved his hands to cup her face and waited for her eyes to open. Her eyelashes fluttered, slowly rising to reveal eyes gone black with arousal. A small outer rim of blue was the only glimpse of her normally clear-blue gaze. When her tongue peaked out and swiped across her kiss-swollen bottom lip, he wanted to dive right back in again. But he couldn't. Not without her full agreement.

"If we're going to stop it has to be now," he growled through clenched teeth. "If you want to keep going then we're moving this party to your bed where I can spread you out and take my fill before starting all over again at the beginning."

Kelsey's breath hitched and she curled her fingers into his shirt tighter as her eyes dilated farther. "I…"

West waited for her to finish. She glanced down, air whistling through her teeth as she flexed her fingers on his chest, digging her nails into his pecs. He knew she was looking at his cock. Regardless of the thick denim of his jeans, his width and length were clearly outlined. "What's it gonna be, Kels?"

Gaze still lowered, she shifted forward, kept moving until her sex sat snug against his. He dragged in a breath, clenching his fingers as he used his grip to tilt her face up. Her eyes were alight with lust and a dark swirl of need lanced through his belly and exploded in his groin. He'd given her an out. Done the right thing by giving her a choice, but with that move, with the way she was grinding herself against him…

He pulled her head to his and slanted his mouth over hers. Any answer she might have given was erased by the swipe of his tongue. She met him stroke for stroke. And when he slipped his hands down her neck and over her chest, she tore her mouth from his and arched back.

"Don't stop," she panted.

It was all the invitation West needed. He surged to his feet and, gripping her ass cheeks to keep her wrapped around him, strode from the room.

～

KELSEY'S HEART beat in her chest so hard she thought her ribs might crack. Her stomach fluttered, dipping and rolling, as West carried her down the hall to her room. She knew there were reasons they shouldn't do this. Knew this would complicate their already confusing relationship, but for the life of her she couldn't deny herself the pleasure of being with him again.

He dropped her to the bed and followed her down, draping his hard body over hers and pressing her deeper into the mattress. His weight was a welcome burden. One she'd craved with a secret yearning for years. And now she was here. Beneath him once more.

"Kels."

Her gaze met his.

"This is your last chance. Yes or no?"

His eyes searched hers, the need and desire flaring in the deep-gray gaze she knew so well only reaffirmed her decision. "Yes."

West took her mouth then. But this time he didn't ravish—he cherished. With liquid strokes and barely there caresses, he drove her out of her mind with need. She wanted them naked. Wanted to be under him skin on skin, hard on soft. His mouth left hers to trail over her chin and along her jaw until his lips toyed with the delicate skin beneath her ear. He licked and sucked and nipped with his teeth, drawing unintelligible words from her throat.

Growling, West dragged his teeth across her flesh and latched onto her earlobe. Sucked it between his lips and flicked it with his tongue. A shiver skipped down her spine.

"I want you naked. Now." The gravelly need-drenched tone sent a shudder shaking her from head to toe.

He sprang from the bed and Kelsey watched, unable to move as he put his arms over his head, grabbed the back of his shirt and tugged it off with one swift yank. Her mouth watered. His chest was a work of art. She'd felt his sculptured contours earlier, but seeing them uncovered did extraordinary things to her insides. She tightened and loosened all at once. Slick heat filled her core while the rolling clench of her pussy was a reminder of how long she'd gone without the pleasure of a man between her thighs.

West tipped his chin towards her as his hands worked at the

button on his pants. "Get naked, Kels, or I'm ripping those clothes off you."

She had no doubt he'd follow through on his threat, but suddenly the idea of being exposed to this man delivered a sharp blade of fear she had no hope of squashing when faced with such masculine perfection.

"Kelsey?" West's hands were clenched at his sides, his jeans open but still up, and she brought her gaze up to meet his. "Second thoughts?"

She sank her teeth into her bottom lip as she shook her head.

"I'm hanging on the edge. You're either in this with me, all the way, or you're not."

"You're beautiful." The words left her mouth without consent and her cheeks filled with heat at her wayward tongue.

He grinned and pushed his pants down his hips, revealing his erection. "Oh no." West kicked his pants aside and put one knee on the bed. "We haven't even begun to uncover beautiful yet."

And then he began to undress her. He started with her top. Inching it up her body to reveal a centimeter at a time, he took long seconds to kiss each new section of skin he exposed.

"Here."

He kissed the curve of her waist.

"And here."

Another kiss just below her belly button.

"Mmm, here too."

More kisses were trailed across her stomach until she quivered with anticipation of where he would lay his lips next. It seemed to take forever for him to reach her breasts. But when he did, the attention she was expecting never came. Instead, he trailed his fingers over her, dragging her top with them, up to her collarbones. She trembled as she waited to see what he would do.

"I think we need to get rid of this." West tugged on her shirt, urging her to lift up and raise her arms so he could whisk the fabric away. "Ah, there. See, now that's what I call beautiful."

He stroked his fingers along the lace edge of her bra, his thumbs a whispered caress over her taut nipples where they pressed against the silky barrier that remained between them. Her breath hitched and she held still, every nerve waiting for the next touch, the next word.

"So, so beautiful," he murmured as he lowered his head to press his lips to the upper curve of her breast.

"West." Kelsey wasn't sure what she wanted or how to say it, she just knew she needed him to do more. Yes. "More."

His mouth found hers and he spoke against her lips. "Don't worry. There's definitely going to be more. But first..." He sat up and moved lower on the bed. "These have to go."

He slid his fingers into either side of her sweat pants and tugged them down her legs. She held her breath as he stared down at the sheer white panties she wore. They were one of her nicest pairs and she briefly wondered if she'd put them on yesterday with this in mind.

"God. Kelsey."

Her fears of earlier evaporated under his gaze, in the echo of his words. In that moment, she believed he saw her as beautiful whether she saw herself that way or not. She curled her hands around his biceps and pulled him closer as she lifted up to meet him. When her mouth met his, she nibbled on his lips, licked at the seam and pressed inside to taste him again.

He let her have her way, held perfectly still while letting her lead him into the sweetest kiss she'd ever known. As the seconds ticked by, Kelsey's need grew until kissing him wasn't enough. She had to have it all.

7

———

Weest pulled in a sharp breath and stared at the woman laid out before him. She'd been gorgeous as a teenager but now...with all the curves the years had added, Kelsey was a mouthwatering, mind-numbing dream come true. *His* dream come true. He wanted to devour her—gobble her up whole—and slake the lust burning in his bones. Except he didn't want to rush—didn't want this to be over too soon. Like their first time, he wanted to take his time, imprint every second of being with her on his memory for all eternity.

He traced a finger along the edge of her underwear. Back and forth. Back and forth. When he dipped beneath the flimsy fabric, she sucked in a breath, her stomach rippling, as he teased the skin hidden but not. The sheerness of her lace panties really didn't conceal a thing. Her dark cleft was easily seen and the moisture seeping from her body rendered the crotch area completely transparent. But even with so little of her covered, he wanted to see more.

"Let's get rid of these." West slipped both hands into the sides of her underwear and dragged them over her hips and down her thighs. "Jesus."

If he thought the sight of her wet panties was a turn on, it was

56

nothing compared to the glistening flesh he'd revealed. His hands shook as he pulled her pants the rest of the way off. He tossed them over his shoulder, uncaring of where they landed, and then he reached for her hands and tugged her up until she sat before him so he could get rid of the last barrier between them.

"And this." With one flick, he had her bra undone. The straps slipped from her shoulders and he didn't waste a second removing it from her body and throwing it aside. "Jesus. You're so beautiful."

He pushed her back onto the bed as he leaned over and dropped a kiss on her stomach, just below her belly button and the cute little belly ring he'd had no idea she'd gotten. With his tongue, he toyed with the dangling stone and watched as goose bumps rose in a wave over her skin.

"When did you get this?" he spoke while continuing to tease her with his lips, his tongue and finally, his teeth, giving the tiny silver chain that held the sparkling purple stone a tug.

"A-ages. Ago." Her words came out around her stuttered breath and West smiled against her skin as he nuzzled his way higher.

"I like it," he murmured against the underside of her breast. "A lot." He nipped her smooth skin.

Her breath hitched, her chest rising and offering him the perfect place to feast. He didn't need to be enticed by her curves though. He was already well aware of—and wanted—every part of her. He'd waited so long to get her here. To be hovering over her while she quivered beneath him. And as much as he wanted to take his time, his patience to have her was running out. Fast.

West ran his tongue up between Kelsey's breasts until he reached the hollow at the base of her throat. Her pulse beat frantically beneath her skin and he figured if that was an indication of her arousal, she was right there with him. On the verge of going over the edge with little encouragement. Did she want him as badly as he wanted her? God, he hoped so. Because at this point, he wasn't fooling himself any longer. He had to have her and have her now.

"Kels." He spoke her name but he couldn't decide if he was asking for something or just reminding himself of who he was with—that this wasn't a dream like so many times before.

"West. Please."

He pulled back enough to look at her face, to see her eyes and the need and the want swirling in her gaze. To confirm in his own mind that he wasn't the only one being driven crazy. "Tell me what you want?"

West wasn't sure why he asked her, because he didn't think he could last much longer. If she didn't want what he did…

Kelsey cupped his face with both hands and pulled him towards her until their mouths were a breath apart. "You. I want you."

Her words were exactly what he needed to hear. With a slowness that almost killed him, West lowered his body to hers. From toes to chest, he pressed himself against her. His cock found the soft cushion of her pussy and the heat and wetness that surrounded his throbbing flesh dragged a groan from his throat.

"I want you now. *Need* you now."

"Yes," she breathed against his mouth before her lips met his.

The kiss started out soft—sweet—but soon their tongues tangled and their teeth bumped as they ate hungrily at each other. West rocked his hips, his intentions clear, and when Kels arched up to join him in their intimate dance, he knew he'd reached his limit.

He tore his mouth from hers. "Protection?"

"I'm covered and clean." She chewed the corner of her mouth and West's balls throbbed.

"I'm clean, but I have a condom in my wallet if you want me to get it." He had to give her the option. She had no reason to believe him, and while he hadn't been with a woman since he'd heard her and Bry had split, Kels didn't know that, and West had no intention of telling her. Yet. Giving her that kind of power over him when this thing between them was so fresh didn't feel right.

Her eyes searched his and West thought she might have been having second thoughts about the whole thing. In a split second, he made the decision for her. As much as he wanted to take her bare, he wanted her to want that too, and right now he wasn't sure she wanted him to keep going never mind come inside her.

"I'll grab the condom."

West jumped off the bed and raced from the room, cursing under his breath the whole way to the kitchen for taking his wallet out of his back pocket. He found his keys on the counter but no wallet. He could have sworn he'd put them down together. Spinning around, he was about to make his way to the living room when he kicked the missing wallet across the floor. It must have dropped off the counter at some point last night.

He scooped it up and ran back to the bedroom. It probably looked odd, a naked man sprinting through the house, but at this point West didn't care. All he was worried about was getting back to Kelsey before she changed her mind. Flipping his wallet open, he pulled out the one condom he kept on hand and prayed it wasn't past its use-by date. Although she said she was covered, he still didn't want to deal with the stress a broken condom would cause when they already had enough tension in their relationship.

"Got it." He held it up as he re-entered Kelsey's room, stopping short when he caught sight of her.

She hadn't moved. Her legs were stretched out, slightly parted and her hands rested on the pillow beside her head. She really was his dream come to life, and with everything he was, he would make sure he didn't fuck things up this time.

Forcing himself to move, West made his way back to the bed, dropping his wallet and tearing open the foil packet as he went. He stood at the foot of the mattress looking up at Kelsey, his gaze locked on hers as he fitted the condom over his cock. Covered, he placed a hand either side of her legs and slowly climbed onto the bed and up her body until his mouth hovered over hers.

"You still with me?" He wanted to kick his own ass for giving her another out, but he needed her with him. All the way with him.

"Yes." She placed her hands on his chest and trailed them down his torso until he shuddered with anticipation of her fingers wrapping around his hard length. Except she didn't grab him. Instead, she slid her hands to his hips and, digging in her fingers, urged him down.

He complied because he had no choice. His mind was one step behind his body. Slipping a knee between hers, West nudged until Kels parted her legs farther and gave him the room he needed to settle over her completely. They fit perfectly. At least it seemed that way to him. Then again, he'd waited so long to be with her he wouldn't care even if they didn't match in all the right places.

When they finally connected, skin to skin, from chest to feet, he held still. He wanted to take one second—only one—to savor the feel of Kels beneath him. She was soft where he was hard, and the silkiness of her skin where it pressed against his made him think of warm honey. Why, he hadn't a clue, but think it he did.

This woman did things to him no one else ever had. It wasn't just his body that reacted to her, his mind did too, thoughts and ideas inspired by nobody but Kelsey always filled his head when she was around. And when she wasn't. He'd never wanted to do better, *be* better, for anybody but her. If she'd only give him a chance, he'd spend the rest of his life being the best at everything for her.

KELSEY DIDN'T THINK she'd drawn a full breath since West had taken off her clothes. The way he'd cherished each new section of flesh he'd uncovered and those teasing tugs on her belly ring had stolen her ability to think as well as breathe. He made her feel sexy and beautiful and desirable in a way Bry never had. Not that she should or was comparing them. They were so different and not just in the way they made her feel.

Bry was safe, comfortable, like slipping on a pair of old running shoes. Whereas West was daring, sexy beyond belief and a little disturbing, like wearing a pair of five-inch red stilettos. Except there were moments when West made her feel so content to be near him that she had to wonder if he couldn't give her what she'd sought from Bry all those years ago. Why she was thinking any of this while they lay skin on skin for the first time in over a decade was anyone's guess.

She didn't need to worry about thinking anymore when West bucked his hips and distracted her with the hot, heavy slide of his cock over her sex. Her muscles contracted and moisture coated her folds as the area throbbed with need. She'd never felt this close to coming with so little stimulation. It always took concentration on her part—concerted effort on her partner's—to get her there.

Except with West.

With him, all it took was a look. Kelsey didn't know whether to be embarrassed by how easy she was where he was concerned or thrilled that he could give her pleasure without thought or effort. Not wanting to be the only one experiencing this almost overwhelming rush to the finish line, she set her hands and fingers in motion. She started with his back and explored the smooth contours of muscle over bone, the broad sweep of his shoulders and then down his spine to the taut globes of his ass.

"God. That feels so good. Don't stop, Kels. Touch me everywhere."

West's panted words urged her on. She wanted to stroke every inch of him, but the need pulsing between her thighs grew more demanding with each beat, and she knew touching him wasn't going to be enough. Not right now.

Kelsey rolled her hips, thrust up and down with an urgency that increased the more she did it. His legs slipped deeper between hers and the crown of his cock nestled its way inside her folds to nudge her opening. On reflex, her legs widened and her pelvis lifted, causing him to sink inside the barest of millimeters. But it was enough to send her into a need so frenzied her vision blurred, her hips bucked and her nails dug into the flesh of his ass cheeks.

"Kels. Slow down."

"No." She dug her fingers in harder, used her feet to brace herself against the bed and drove herself onto his length as far as she could.

"Fuck!"

It was the only warning she got before West plunged down and impaled her completely.

For a split second, they froze. Kelsey didn't even breathe. Then everything happened at once. West moved, withdrew on a slow glide that instantly picked up speed, then drove back in again. She rose to meet him, digging her feet into the mattress as she did. He surged in and out, each stroke harder and faster than the last until she had no choice but to just hold on for the ride.

She wrapped her legs around his hips, her arms around his shoulders, and bowed her back to lift her hips to his. The new position sent him deeper, and the change of angle meant his cock brushed over the sensitive spot inside that guaranteed she'd find release.

He rose onto his elbows and stared down at her with eyes gone black. His jaw was firm, a muscle twitched along the right side, and his nostrils flared wide as he drew in ragged breaths.

"I want you with me," he puffed out. "I can't last much longer."

Kelsey wasn't worried he'd come without her. The tightness in her lower belly and the pulsing tingle in her clit signaled she wouldn't last much longer either. And when West leaned to one side and slipped a hand between them to stroke the bundle of nerves gone taut with need, he barely had to touch her to send her flying.

The orgasm ripped through her. It wasn't a gradual wave of release. It was a full-body slam. Head to toe in one simultaneous discharge of energy. Her back arched as every part of her went rigid for a split second before she dissolved into a liquid heat so intense she lost touch with reality for a moment.

West's control seemed to snap in that instant. He grabbed the back of her thighs and pulled them wider as he pistoned his hips, plunging his cock in and out until he broke. His body jerked, his rhythm lost as he came. The growl he emitted through clenched teeth was one of pleasure and pain that she remembered from their first time.

Memories swamped her, and with her emotions so recently bombarded, Kelsey couldn't fight the tears stinging her eyes. They leaked from the corners even though she squeezed her eyes shut so tight she saw stars.

"Kelsey?" West's voice was hoarse.

She didn't open her eyes. Couldn't let him see the regret and longing—the guilt—she knew would be reflected there. Turning her head, she burrowed her face against his neck. He still covered her, remained buried inside, but he held his weight on his arms as he bracketed her head with his hands and forced her to face him.

"Open your eyes." His hands tightened, but not painfully. "Look at me. Please."

It was the please that got her. Slowly, she raised her eyelids and met his gaze.

"Did I hurt you?"

Kelsey shook her head.

"Then why are you crying? Do you regret what we just did already?"

Why did he sound like he expected her to regret this? Even if she had to wait another ten years, or worse, never touched him again, she'd never regret making love with West. "No."

"Then why the tears? Talk to me."

She wasn't sure herself so how could she explain to him the maelstrom of emotions currently turning her insides into a tornado?

WEST EASED out of Kelsey and rolled to the side, taking her with him so she lay across his chest, her head resting on his shoulder. "Talk to me," he murmured into her hair.

He stroked his hands up and down her back, the action designed to soothe her and the sudden anxiety that he'd fucked up royally—again—ripping through his gut.

"Kels?"

She shifted, buried her face against his neck, drew in a deep breath and let it out in a rush. "I don't know."

Huh? "You don't know why you're crying?" How could she not know?

She shook her head, the soft strands of her hair tickling his chin, catching in his stubble.

"Something must have made you cry. Are you sure I didn't hurt you? I was a little rough." He'd been desperate at the end there, and he was afraid his need had caused him to take her too hard—push her too far.

"No. You didn't hurt me." Kelsey tried to pull away but he tightened his grip and held her close.

"Stay. Let me hold you a little while."

West held his breath until she relaxed against him. He didn't speak, didn't want to risk her bolting if he said the wrong thing. He'd wait her out. She'd talk to him eventually. At least he hoped she would.

The phone beside the bed rang, disturbing the strained silence surrounding them. Kelsey pressed her hand to his chest and pushed, but he didn't let her go.

"I should get that," she said, her lips moving over his skin and sending chills down his spine.

"Let your machine pick it up." West wanted to wrap his hands around the neck of the person on the other end of the phone. "It's barely daylight. Who the hell rings at this time of the morning?"

"Nobody. Which is why I should answer. It could be an emergency."

There was nothing urgent enough other than death to warrant a dawn phone call, but he conceded her point. "Maybe. If they leave a message and it is, you can get back to them. If not we can stay right where we are."

Kelsey's voice echoed down the hallway and into the room, her message short and to the point, followed by the beep and then the last person West wanted to hear today of all days spoke.

"Kelsey. Sorry to ring so early, but I knew you wouldn't mind. Mum had a bad night. She's confused and asking for you. She won't let anyone else near her. Do you think you can drop into the home and settle her down this morning? She doesn't recognize me or I'd calm her myself. If you get this in the next thirty minutes ring me." The house went as silent as a tomb when Bry hung up.

Kelsey had stiffened in West's arms the second Bry's voice had blasted through the machine, and West knew there would be nothing he could do or say right now that would do him any favors. So when she pushed out of his arms and turned away to fling her legs off the bed and stand, he let her go without a fight.

"I have to go." She didn't look at him as she made her way over to the bathroom.

"I know." He sat up, removed the condom hanging from his now limp dick and wrapped it in a tissue from the box beside the bed.

"Can you let yourself out?" she asked without turning around.

He'd been dismissed. And while that possibility had lurked in the back of his mind, to actually hear Kels say those words—to *see* her dismiss him without a second thought as she ran to help her ex—cut so deeply that West looked down to check there wasn't a gaping hole in his gut. She was the only person who could kill him with a few words or none at all.

"West?"

He glanced up and met her gaze. "Yeah, I'll let myself out."

There must have been something in his voice or his expression, because she came back to the bed and reached out to stroke her fingers through his hair. "I have to go. Marjorie needs—"

West reached up and placed two fingers over her lips. "It's okay. Go. I'll talk to you later."

"Are you sure?" She spoke against his fingers, the warmth of her breath caressing his skin sending a shiver down his spine.

"Yes." He removed his hand and used both hands on her hips to turn her around and point her in the direction of the bathroom again. "Go. Do what you have to."

She glanced over her shoulder once before nodding and making her way across the room again. When the door closed between them, West let out a breath and flopped back on the bed. He stared at the ceiling. This wasn't the way he wanted to end their first time together, but he couldn't demand she not go no matter how much he wanted to. He'd love to stay until she came out of the bathroom except he didn't think that would do his cause any good either.

With a sigh, he dragged himself off the bed and gathered up his clothes and wallet. He grabbed the used condom and headed to the kitchen where he quickly trashed the rubber, got dressed and scooped up his keys. His shoes were in the living room, and once he had those on he was out of reasons not to leave. Heart heavy in his chest, he made his way to the front door. But he couldn't resist one last glance down the hallway before he opened the door and walked out.

8

Kelsey rushed into the nursing home where Bry met her before she'd taken more than three steps into the foyer.

"Thank God, you're here," he said as he reached for her hand and pulled her into a quick hug.

"How is she?" Kelsey asked as she slipped from his embrace.

"Not good." He led her down the brightly lit hallway. "They were going to sedate her if you didn't get here soon."

"I got here as quickly as I could." Guilt swamped her.

"Oh, I know, I wasn't having a go at you." Bry glanced at her. "Did I wake you?"

"Ah, no. I was up." Kelsey felt her cheeks heat as she recalled exactly what she'd been doing when he rang. "I was, um, in the shower."

"Right. Well, I'm just so grateful that you came." He stopped her outside his mother's room and Kelsey could hear the older woman calling her name from the other side of the closed door, but Bry grabbed her hand before she could push her way inside. "Wait a second. When was the last time you saw mum?"

She had to think for a moment. She'd meant to keep up her visits when she'd separated from Bry, and she had in the beginning, but with setting up her new life and the fact that Marjorie rarely remembered anyone now days, Kelsey had let those visits slide. "A couple of months." She winced. "Maybe six."

"Try not to be shocked by her appearance. She's deteriorated rapidly in the last few weeks. Her weight is down and her lucid episodes are more and more infrequent."

"Okay."

Bry sighed. "She thinks we're still married, Kelsey."

"Oh." The last time she'd seen Marjorie they'd spoken about the divorce and Marjorie had voiced her disappointment that Bry and Kelsey couldn't make it work. Maybe her lack of memory was a good thing. At least now her ex-mother-in-law wouldn't be sad to see her.

"I know it's a lot to ask, but could you pretend we are while you're in there? She doesn't recognize me, so it's not like you'll have to be all over me or anything like that," he quickly reassured her. "In fact, she thinks I'm a doctor who's going to give her some horrible medicine or do something heinous to her so I won't come in at all if that's all right with you."

Kelsey looked at Bry for the first time since she arrived. *Really* looked at him. His cheeks were hollow and the bags under his eyes were a deep, dark-blue-black that made him look as though he hadn't slept in weeks. He'd lost weight too. She placed her hand on his arm and gave him a gentle squeeze. "It's fine. I'll see if I can get her settled."

"Thank you." His smile was a bare stretch of his lips and failed to convey any real happiness.

She smiled a sad smile of her own as she let go and turned to face his mother's door. Taking a deep breath, Kelsey tried to calm her nerves and put a genuine smile on her face. With her emotions fortified and her game face on she pushed open the door and greeted the woman who'd been her surrogate mother for most of her adult life.

"Marjorie. I hear you're giving everyone a hard time."

"Kelsey? Where have you been?" Her former mother-in-law demanded as she rushed towards Kelsey and threw her thin arms around Kelsey's neck.

Kelsey did the only thing she could. She slipped her own arms around Marjorie's frail body and pulled her close. Closing her eyes, she held on, comforting herself and the older woman for long moments.

When Kelsey opened her eyes, she saw the staff had left them alone at some point, and with care, she eased Marjorie out of her arms and over to the bed. "Come on. Let's get you back into bed."

"Where's that son of mine? Why isn't he here with you? I don't know why you ever married that no good fool, but I'm so glad that you did, because if it wasn't for you I'd never see anyone besides those horrible doctors and nurses who want to perform weird medical experiments on me." Marjorie complained the whole time Kelsey helped her onto the bed and tucked her in.

"They're not going to experiment on you. They're trying to make you feel better, not worse," Kelsey soothed.

"Hmph. That's what they tell *you*," Marjorie mumbled as she snuggled down under the blankets.

Kelsey smiled. Marjorie's memory might have gone, but her imagination was still as fanciful as when she'd been a young woman writing fiction novels.

"Want me to read to you?" Kelsey knew that was one thing that her former mother-in-law still enjoyed even in her deteriorated mental state. Well, at least she had when Kelsey had been here last.

"Oh. Yes. Read to me."

The book on Marjorie's bedside table had a bookmark sticking out of the middle. When Kelsey picked it up she discovered someone —probably Bry—had been reading Marjorie one of her own early works. Smiling, she dragged over the armchair and took a seat. "I'll start where you finished off."

She was barely a page in when Marjorie's eyelids started to droop. And by the time Kelsey got to the bottom of the third page, Marjorie was sound asleep. Not wanting to risk stopping too soon, she kept reading for a few more pages.

The door creaked open behind her and she turned to see Bry

poking his head through the small opening. "She asleep?" he whispered.

"Yeah." Kelsey placed the bookmark back where she'd started to read, figuring Marjorie wouldn't remember her reading that part and stood. "We should leave her to rest."

Bry backed out into the hallway as Kelsey moved towards the door. With one final look over her shoulder to assure herself Marjorie was covered, Kelsey exited the room, making sure the door didn't make a sound as it closed behind her. Neither of them spoke as they made their way along the corridor to the family room set aside for residents and their guests.

"Thank you for coming," Bry said as he held the door open for her.

"Bry why didn't you tell me she was getting worse?" Kelsey hoped their divorce hadn't given him the impression she no longer cared about his mother. Or him.

He sighed. "I didn't want to impose."

"Bryan. For God's sake, she's more of a mother to me than my own." It hurt to think he hadn't wanted to share Marjorie's worsening state with her. They might be divorced, but they were still friends. At least she'd thought they were. "I didn't think the divorce had affected our friendship but obviously it has."

"It hasn't." He scrubbed a hand over his face. "I haven't told anyone she's gotten worse. Honestly, until today it was just more prolonged memory loss." Bry shook his head. "I don't know what this morning was about."

Kelsey watched as he dropped into a chair and, resting his elbows on his knees, cradled his head in his hands. She walked over and put her hand on his shoulder. "So what happened last night?"

He shook his head again. "I haven't a clue. The night staff said she went to bed at her usual time. Perfectly fine. Then around one she woke disorientated and calling for you."

She took the seat next to him. "Has something happened recently that might have triggered her memories of me? As I said before, it's probably six months since I've visited and she barely recognized me the last time I was here. I had to keep reminding her who I was."

"No, nothing that I know of. And she hasn't recognized me for the last month, although until today she was happy to sit and chat, let me read to her, but for some reason I'm the enemy now."

Bry sounded so dejected, so heartbroken, that it was only natural for Kelsey to lean over and wrap her arms around him. "I'm so sorry. It's horrible to see Marjorie in such a debilitated state. I can only imagine what it must be like for you."

His arms came around her and he pulled her closer until she was almost in his lap. The action felt so normal, Kelsey didn't think to protest, never mind hold back. She slipped into his lap and held him tight.

"I have no right to ask," Bry murmured into her hair. "But I'm going to. I can't do this on my own any more. I need you, Kelsey."

WEST DROPPED the knife after he narrowly avoided slicing his thumb for the third time. He really shouldn't be chopping onions when his mind wasn't completely focused on the job. He'd be lucky if he didn't lose a finger, never mind cut one. With a sigh, he left the knife where it had fallen and walked over to the cold room to grab a bottle of water. Bottle in hand, he headed for his office. The onions could wait. It was busy work anyway.

No one else was in yet, the quiet only broken by the hum of the refrigeration units, and he knew he had the place to himself for another couple of hours. Plenty of time to brood. Alone.

He'd gone home after leaving Kelsey's, but a shower hadn't calmed his agitated state so he'd headed in to work. Not that he'd fared much better here. He dropped into his chair and leaned back, closing his eyes. It wasn't even three hours since he'd left Kels, but he already craved the sight—the touch—of her again.

She hadn't called to let him know everything was okay. Then again, should he expect her to? Sure, they'd slept together, but did that mean they were supposed to check in now? He didn't think so. And if recent weeks—hell, months—were anything to go by, he'd be the one making the first move. Every time he'd gotten closer, she'd thrown up a red light to stop him. He didn't think the fact they'd finally tumbled into bed would make any difference either. His phone vibrated in his pocket and his heart skipped a beat in hope. Hope that was quickly crushed when he saw the message was from Coop.

Can't make tonight.

Tonight? West's mind went blank. He had no idea what Coop was referring to. He started to type a reply when it hit him. They were supposed to get together with Zac for a few drinks. He deleted what he'd already written and started again.

Cool. Works for me. You wanna text Zac or will I?

West held his phone and waited for Coop to reply. Instead, he got a message from Zac.

Don't tell me. Something came up for you too.

He stared at his phone. He could hear the censure in his friend's words. West thought about saying yes but decided he really needed to get whatever the hell was bugging Zac out in the open before it destroyed their friendship.

Nope. I'm still good. Usual time, usual place?

He'd just hit send when his phone buzzed again. Coop.

WTF is up with Zac!!

West smiled. At least he wasn't the only one on the receiving end of Zac's mood. Thumbs flying over the screen, West fired off a reply to Coop.

No idea but I plan to find out. Going ahead with tonight. I'll let you know what happens.

He didn't have a clue when he'd see Kelsey now. Mentally going over this afternoon's schedule, West figured he could get away a few hours early and catch her at home. If she *was* home. Glancing at the time, West decided to ring her and see if she wanted to grab an early dinner with him before he met up with Zac. His phone went off twice in rapid succession before he could open his contacts. The first was from Zac.

Sure. Same time, same place.

The second from Coop.

Good luck. Wear a flak jacket.

West grinned. Hopefully, he wouldn't need armor when he saw Zac. Although West had the feeling his heart could probably do with some protection when it came to Kelsey. He wasn't the type of guy to put things off except when it came to her. But he wouldn't let his irrational fear of all things Kels get the better of him. He'd made the decision to pursue so he'd man up and do what he had to. Hitting speed-dial one, he brought the phone to his ear and waited for Kels to answer.

It rang five times before she picked up. "Hello?" Her breathless voice whispered in his ear, reminding him of the way she'd breathed his name earlier when they were in bed and he was driving her—himself—crazy.

He swallowed to wet his suddenly parched throat. "Hey. How'd it go?" West asked about Bry's mother even though he wanted desperately to get to the more important topic. Them.

"Um, good. Can I call you back? I'm in the middle of something."

"Oh, sure." West bit his tongue to stop the question of when from popping out his mouth.

"I don't know how long I'll be." He heard someone call her in the background. "I gotta go. I'll call you."

Right before she hung up West heard the same voice calling out again and a ball of lead sank to the pit of his stomach. He didn't want to believe what his ears, and mind, were telling him, but even if it were true there had to be a perfectly good explanation as to what Kelsey was doing all out of breath with her ex-husband. Shame he didn't think even a legitimate reason for them being together was acceptable.

~

"Who was that?"

Kelsey spun around to find Bry had followed her into the kitchen. "Huh?"

"On the phone." He tipped his chin to indicate the device still in her hand. "Client?"

"Client?" Her mind still played the reel of memories hearing West's voice had conjured up, making it hard to focus on the conversation.

Bry ginned. "Obviously not a client if you're this flustered. Boyfriend?"

"Wh-what?" She choked on the breath she'd just inhaled. Her cheeks heated, making her bring her hands up to cover her face while she continued to hack and splutter.

Kelsey spun around and grabbed a glass from the cupboard. She quickly filled it with water and took a sip, trying to soothe the rawness her coughing fit left behind.

"Hey. You okay?" Bry came up behind her, placed his hands on her shoulders and turned her around. "Come sit down."

She let him guide her to a chair and dropped into it, relieved to not be standing on her shaky legs any longer. He'd thrown her with the boyfriend comment. They'd never talked about dating others. Actually, Kelsey had never even contemplated dating, either her or Bry. Now though, she could only conclude that if he thought she was seeing someone then it was possible he was.

The stab of jealously Kelsey thought she should feel never happened. All she felt at the idea of Bry moving on with someone else was relief. Which delivered a shaft of guilt. She should never have married him. Should never have promised to love above all others when she'd known she couldn't.

"Better now?"

His words snapped her out of her thoughts. "Oh, yes. Breathed the wrong way, I guess." She shrugged and took another sip of water.

"Are you sure? 'Cause I should get going, but I don't want to leave you if you're not all right."

"I'm fine. Go." Kelsey gave him a little push. "I have to get to work anyway."

"Thanks again for this morning." Bry leaned down and kissed her forehead. "And for everything else you've agreed to."

Kelsey smiled up at the man she'd married—the man she still held great affection for—and wished with all her heart that it could have been different between them. "No need to thank me, Bry. I'm more than happy to help out with Marjorie."

For the first time since she'd seen him this morning his mouth curved in a genuine smile. "You might be happy to but you're not obligated, so I still feel the need to thank you. Probably will forever."

Kelsey frowned. "It's really not necessary."

"I know. And that's what I love about you, Kelsey. You're always willing to go above and beyond." He stroked a finger down her cheek, but unlike West's touch, there was no firing of neurons. No zap of desire hitting her veins. "I'll see you tonight."

"Yep. Six o'clock." She pushed out of the chair and followed him out of her kitchen.

"I'll bring take-out for dinner so we can eat before we head over to see mum."

"Sounds good." Kelsey held the front door wide as Bry stepped outside. "Oh, and, Bry. Try not to worry too much. Marjorie is getting the best of care at the home and everything that can be done is being done to make her comfortable."

He glanced over his shoulder. "I know. Having you with me makes it all easier to cope with too."

A twinge of guilt hit Kelsey, tightening her stomach. She'd let him and Marjorie down with her neglect. She wouldn't do that again. "I'm here for whatever you need."

"Thanks." Bry waved as he made his way down the path to the kerb where he'd parked his car when he'd followed her home to talk about Marjorie's situation.

Kelsey watched until he'd driven down the street and out of sight. She closed the door and then made her way back to the kitchen and her phone. She'd left it on the counter, and as much as she wanted to put off the coming conversation, she couldn't. She had to return West's call.

9

Every muscle in West's body tightened when he glanced at his ringing phone. He stared at it through three rings with trepidation tugging at his gut.

Kelsey.

He'd anticipated this call with a mixture of excitement and dread. Surprise ricocheted through him at the sight of his shaking hand and he swiped his thumb across the screen with a little too much force, making him juggle it as he brought it up to his ear.

"Kels."

He heard her suck in a deep breath before the voice that had called out in pleasure only hours ago echoed in his ear. "Hey, I can talk now."

For a split second, West had the urge to say he couldn't, but the notion was quickly overtaken by the need that burned in his bones for this woman. "You okay?"

"Of course. Why wouldn't I be?" He could picture her scrunching up her nose in question.

"You sounded weird earlier. I thought something might be wrong, that's all." His gut clenched when he thought about how out of breath she'd sounded and how it reminded him of making her breathless with satisfaction this morning. He quickly changed the subject. As much as he wanted to know what had gone on between her and Bry, he didn't. "Anyway, I've got a few hours tonight before I have to meet Zac, so I thought I'd bring dinner to your place around six."

"Oh. I can't."

"Seven then?" He'd be pushing it to make it, but for Kels he'd risk Zac's wrath by being a few minutes late.

"Ah, it's not really a good night—"

"Don't cut me out again, Kels." West couldn't stand it if she avoided him like she had in the past.

Her sigh filled his ear before she said the words he'd longed to hear. "I'm not, but I've got stuff going on, plus you're expecting to see me in the office next week, and at this rate I'll never clear all my clients off my desk."

"I told you you could see them out of here." West didn't want to give her any reason to quit before she started. "There isn't enough work here to fill your days, so it makes sense to continue to run your business out of my office."

"West." Her exasperation came through loud and clear.

"What? Surely you can see this is a mutually beneficial arrangement." He leaned against the counter and rubbed his fingers back and forth on his forehead. "C'mon, Kels. You and I both know you can do the office managers job in your sleep. There's no need for you to rush any of your clients' work."

She sucked in a breath. "I really can't see you tonight."

That pulled him up short, making his back straighten and his heart sink. "Why?" He knew before she spoke, but he hoped—

"Bry is coming over."

When her words met his ear, he clenched his jaw and ground his back teeth together. "Fuck."

"It's not what you think." Her words rushed over each other.

"And what is it I think, Kels?" Jealousy and anger burned in his gut.

"We're deciding on how best to handle Marjorie's worsening health."

"*We?* Why the fuck is it *we*? You're divorced. I know you were with him for years, but you don't owe him or his mother any kind of loyalty." West could hear the words he was saying. Knew they were callous and heartless. But he didn't care. His hurt and frustration were blinding him to his selfish behavior. Just when he thought he'd made it past Kelsey's red lights, he found himself faced with another one.

"West, please understand. Marjorie gave me what my own mother has never been able to. Whether I owe her or Bry doesn't come into it. She's someone I care about. Someone I want to support during this difficult time. God knows how much longer she'll be with us, and if I can help make that time a little better I will."

Suitably chastised, he closed his eyes, took a deep breath and tried to reel in his chaotic emotions. If he didn't gain control, she'd push him away again. "I get that, I do. But you can't hold the fact I want to see you against me. You have to know this morning wasn't just about sex for me."

West gripped the phone tighter as he waited for her to say something. Silence stretched until he thought the connection had been cut off. On the verge of pulling the phone from his ear to check, she spoke.

"It wasn't just sex for me either."

Thank God.

"But I can't deal with this—*us*—today."

Damn. That wasn't what he wanted to hear. "How long?"

"I, I don't know. This thing with Bry isn't going to be a one-time deal. It'll be ongoing. I'm sorry. I *need* to do this."

He understood Kelsey's need to help others. It was her doing so above her own needs and wants that he couldn't wrap his head around. She was the least selfish person he'd ever met, always looking out for those around her. West knew it came from her childhood. Having to take care of her younger siblings while her mother hid in the bottom of a bottle had left a mark. All he wanted to do was take care of her, make sure she got what she needed—wanted. If she'd let him.

"Can I call you later? After you've dealt with your commitments."

West needed a definite time of when they'd connect next even if it was only by phone. He needed to have her with him on this or at least know where they stood, and to do that they had to talk.

"Sure. I'll text you after I'm back from visiting Marjorie tonight."

It was better than nothing, and really, he had no choice but to accept the small concession for now. He'd prefer in person, but at this point he'd take whatever the hell he could get. "We'll talk later then."

"Okay. Oh, and, West?"

"Yeah."

"Could we keep what happened this morning just between us?"

"I'm not about to brag about getting you into bed, Kelsey."

"I didn't think you were, but I'd rather no one know right at the moment. It's not like we know what it is we're doing."

And there it was. While Kelsey wasn't sure what was going on between them West had a crystal-clear view of their future. It involved white picket fences and happy ever afters. But the last thing he wanted to do was scare her off with his plans. "Fine. Just between us."

For now.

Kelsey tapped out a message to West. He wouldn't be happy when he read it, but there was nothing she could do about it. Marjorie was far more agitated than she'd been this morning, and even though they'd had to resort to sedating Bry's mother, Kelsey couldn't bring herself to leave her former mother-in-law just yet—or leave Bry to deal with it on his own. Bry had suggested she leave the room while they administered the medication so Marjorie wouldn't lose faith in the only person she seemed to trust in her confused world.

She could hear Marjorie calling for her and it took all the strength Kelsey had not to go back in there before the nurses and doctor came out. Poor Bry had been relegated to doctor again and therefore one of the bad guys. It saddened Kelsey to see the woman who'd loved her son dearly not recognize him at all anymore. Kelsey wasn't sure how Bry coped with the blank stare his mother now gave him. They'd had such a close relationship, especially after Bry's father had passed away.

Her phone vibrated in her hand. Opening the message, she braced herself for West's anger. But it never came. Instead, he gave her something she hadn't realized she needed. Acceptance.

Do what you need to. Ring me when you're done. Doesn't matter how late. I'll wait up.

It was already after eleven and Kelsey wasn't sure how long the sedation would take to work, but she didn't think she'd be home before midnight. She stifled a yawn as she replied.

It'll be after twelve.

Funny how she hadn't wanted to face West after this morning and now she wanted to cling to this connection with both hands.

I'll be here.

She closed her eyes and leaned her head against the wall. Exhaustion had dug its claws in hours ago, but seeing Marjorie in full-blown panic when they'd arrived and not being able to do anything to calm the older woman had ripped what was left of her energy away. Kelsey had to admit she was glad Bry had talked her into riding over with him. At least now she wouldn't be a hazard on the road on the way home.

"Kelsey?"

Her eyes popped open and she jerked away from the wall, turning in Bry's direction. "Is she okay?" She rushed forward—if dragging her feet could be called rushing.

He scrubbed a hand down his face. "Yeah. She's already drifting off. I was thinking it might be better if you don't go back in there."

"Oh?"

"You can just tell her you came back after getting a coffee and found her asleep. If we're lucky, she won't remember anything. She certainly didn't recall last night or seeing you this morning." Bry's shoulders sagged and Kelsey couldn't stop herself from reaching out to touch him.

"If you think that's the best way to deal with it." She gently squeezed his arm before letting go.

"Mr. and Mrs. Newman."

Kelsey glanced over Bry's shoulder to see the doctor she'd met earlier coming out of Marjorie's room. She almost stumbled over the stab of fear that sliced through her chest when she saw the concern creasing his face.

"Is Mum okay?" Bry asked as he turned to face the doctor.

"Oh, yes, yes, she's sleeping soundly now." The other man walked towards them, his steps no more energetic than Kelsey's had been. "I just wanted to remind you that Marjorie has a routine doctor's visit tomorrow. I'm a little worried about her recent increase in confusion and anxiety, so I'll be talking to her specialist in the morning about getting her in for a CT scan."

"Why? What are you looking for?" Bry asked, his posture suddenly alert.

Bry slipped his hand into hers and their fingers tangled together naturally. Kelsey tightened her grip to offer her support but didn't say a word. She might be here as his ex-wife and Marjorie's ex-daughter-in-law but she had no real right to ask questions or demand answers.

"I'm not sure. I just want to rule out a few things," the doctor explained.

"Like what?" Bry's grip grew painfully tight and Kelsey wiggled her fingers until he loosened it. "Don't keep me in the dark."

"I'd rather not say anything until I have some solid evidence either way, Mr. Newman."

"Cut the crap, would you? It's been a long day—a long few months—and I'd rather not be blindsided tomorrow."

Kelsey could understand Bry's need to know, but if the doctor was only running on a hunch... "Bry, the doctor's right. It's best not to worry until you have to."

"I can't possibly get any more worried, no matter what he tells me." The strain and exhaustion of dealing with Marjorie's condition were clear in Bry's voice.

The doctor let out a sigh. "Look, I'm running on a tiny bit of instinct here, and I wouldn't normally say a word to the family of a patient, but I know how difficult the last few months have been for you. It's possible, and I stress I'm not sure and won't be until we see medical evidence, but I think you're mother may have suffered a mild stroke in the last few days."

"A stroke? But she doesn't appear to have any symptoms," Bry pointed out.

"Not all strokes are obvious. Unfortunately, a minor one can lead to a major one, and again I'll stress, I just want to rule this out, but I have seen it in elderly patients before."

"What happens if she has had a stroke?" Kelsey couldn't stop herself from asking.

"Let's cross that bridge when we come to it. We're monitoring her closely, and if there's any change in her condition or if I, or one of the staff, are concerned at all, we'll have her transferred straight to the hospital."

Bry let go of Kelsey's hand and extended his to the doctor. "Thank you. And I'm sorry I snapped at you. It's been a tiring few days."

"Totally understand." They shook. "Go on home and get some rest. We'll talk tomorrow."

They watched the doctor walk away and it struck Kelsey as strange that she couldn't remember his name. They'd been introduced earlier, but for the life of her she couldn't recall the man's name. She covered her mouth to hide a yawn she was unable to suppress.

"C'mon. Let's get you home before you fall asleep on your feet." Bry tugged on her hand, pulling her away from Marjorie's room and towards the front entrance. "Thanks for coming tonight."

"Any time." Another yawn cracked her jaw. "Gosh. I really am tired all of a sudden."

"Sorry about tonight. I should have given in earlier and let them sedate Mum instead of spending hours trying to calm her down. Especially when she doesn't even recognize me."

"How long has her memory been this bad?" She didn't want to say it, but basically she was asking how long since his mum had forgotten him.

Bry pushed open the front door and ushered her through. "I had five minutes about two weeks ago. Other than that, it's been well over a month." He pressed his hand to the small of her back and steered her across the parking lot to his car.

"I'm sorry." The sentiment seemed inadequate even if it was genuine, but there wasn't anything else to say in a situation like this.

Bry remained quiet as he unlocked his car. He opened the door and held it while he waited for Kelsey to get settled before speaking again. "I think I have to face the fact that Mum is essentially gone now. The woman we both knew isn't coming back."

Kelsey had no chance to reply before Bry shut the door and circled around the bonnet. He slipped into the driver's seat and started the car without another word.

Talking seemed pointless, so Kelsey leaned her head back and closed her eyes. What felt like seconds later but had to be at least forty-five minutes, she was jolted from a light doze when Bry pulled into her driveway.

"Thanks again for tonight," he said as he put the car in park and pulled on the handbrake.

"You're welcome." She faced him in the dark. The only light came from the glow from the dashboard and it made his tired features appear even more haggard. Kelsey felt ineffectual in her limited support. "Do you want me to come with you to Marjorie's doctor's appointment in the morning?"

"No. And I know we planned for us both to go in tomorrow night again, but it might be better to wait and see what her doctor says."

"Oh, okay."

"I'll call you." He leaned over and kissed her.

It was a quick brush of lips. A kiss between friends, and Kelsey was reminded again of the lack of passion between them. They'd never fired sparks off each other, and the thought made her sad but also made her crave West in ways she'd never wanted her ex-husband. Uncertain in Bry's presence for the first time since their separation and subsequent divorce, Kelsey reached for the door handle.

"Ring me tomorrow if you need me," she said as she pushed the door open and swung her legs out.

"I seem to be saying it a lot, but thanks, Kelsey. You're more generous than you should be."

"Nonsense. This is what friends are for." She tried not to put emphasis on the word friends, but that kiss had set off some warning bells. Kelsey didn't think he had any ideas of them getting back together, but in the three years since they'd gone their separate ways, he'd never kissed her. Not on the mouth. It felt like a line had been crossed. Then again, maybe that was because a small part of her saw that kiss as a betrayal of West.

Before her chaotic thoughts got the better of her, she slipped out of the car and closed the door. Without looking back, Kelsey walked up the path to her house. She retrieved her keys from her pocket and slipped the key into the lock. Giving Bry a quick wave, she opened the door, ducked inside and locked up before making her way to her bedroom where she collapsed onto the bed in complete exhaustion.

WEST LET himself into Kelsey's house. He knew he shouldn't. It was two o'clock in the morning. But she hadn't called him like she'd promised and she hadn't answered her phone the numerous times he'd rung in the last few hours either. No lights were on and he didn't bother with them as he made his way down the short hallway to her room. Moonlight streamed in through the open blinds illuminating the woman sprawled across the bed. She still had her shoes on.

Smiling, he shook his head as he put his keys, wallet and phone on her dresser and walked over to the bed. With care, he picked up one foot and eased her shoe off. She didn't stir so he repeated his actions with the other foot. Shoeless, Kelsey murmured something he didn't catch before rolling over onto her back. West eyed her jeans and debated whether or not to rid her of them. She'd be more comfortable out of them.

But she'd probably pitch a fit if she woke without her clothes, and while he didn't mind getting her riled up, that wasn't the kind of reaction he wanted from her. He dropped to his knees beside the bed. Using his fingertips, he brushed the hair from her face and studied her. In sleep, she looked younger than her twenty-eight years. She reminded him of the girl he'd fallen for in high school.

"Kelsey." He moved his hand to her shoulder and gave her a gentle shake. "Kels."

"Mmm."

"You need to get out of your clothes."

"Mm-kay."

West grinned when she reached for the hem of her shirt and dragged it up her torso. She didn't open her eyes, and while he was okay with receiving an impromptu strip show, he didn't think her intention was to tease him. Before he could say anything to stop her, she'd whipped her top off and went to work on the button of her pants.

"Whoa. Kelsey." He stilled her hands. "Let me get out of the room first." West might have seen her naked already, but it felt as though he'd be crossing a line if he stayed while she undressed. He didn't think she'd be too pleased about it once she was awake enough to comprehend what she'd done either.

"Ss-okay."

He thought she was agreeing with him, but when she continued to undo her jeans and shove them down her hips, he realized she'd meant something completely different.

"Kelsey."

"Can't." She tugged on the denim, revealing a pair of pink lace panties. "Help me." She opened her eyes and the slumberous blue depths met his.

"I..." West couldn't finish the thought never mind the sentence.

"Please."

God help him, he wasn't going to be able to refuse her. He hadn't come here for this. He'd been worried when she hadn't called and had just wanted to check she was all right, not get her naked. West gripped the waistband of her jeans and pulled them down her legs and over her feet while trying his best not to look at the miles of flesh revealed. When he glanced up, she was already working on the front catch of her bra. In the blink of an eye, all that stood between him and her lush curves was a single strip of flimsy pink lace sitting low on her hips.

West swallowed, his constricted throat making it difficult. "Kels." He wasn't sure what he meant to say, but her name fell from his lips a little too pleading for his liking. Clearing his throat he tried again. "Kelsey, you need to get into bed."

Her eyes drifted closed as she reached her arms out towards him. "You too."

"No. I should go." He managed to avoid her by standing, but that left her groping hands right near his groin—the one with the hard-on straining to get out of his pants. West grit his teeth when she grabbed a handful of his sweats—her fingers brushing along his length—and yanked.

Distracted by her touch and surprised by her show of strength, he lost his balance and toppled forward. Throwing his arms out, he caught himself on his hands before he crushed her beneath him. When he looked down, it was to find Kelsey staring at him with eyes soaking in need. And not the kind of need pumping blood into his cock either. What he saw in her eyes was a whole new level of wanting that he'd waited a lifetime to see Kelsey aim his way.

"Please, West. I need you to hold me."

He had no idea what was going on. Why the woman who'd avoided, ignored and rejected him at various points over the last few months suddenly wanted him on a level he'd craved, but he didn't care. His one weakness had always been Kelsey, and he could no more deny her this than he could live the rest of his life without breathing.

Toeing off his shoes, he let them drop to the floor before moving to the center of the bed, taking her with him. He turned her so she lay wrapped in his arms, her head cradled on his shoulder, and held her while she slid back into a deep sleep. West was pretty sure she'd regret this in the morning, whatever the hell this was. But for now, he'd bask in her acceptance. It might not be the confession of love he wanted—needed—from her, but he wasn't above taking whatever he could get.

10

For the second morning in a row, West woke tangled with Kelsey. And Kelsey attempting to make a quiet getaway without much success. Unless her aim was to inflict physical harm. Then she was definitely doing an okay job.

West moved his leg to shield his groin. "You're going to do some real damage if we keep this up," he murmured.

"Shit." Kelsey jolted. Her elbow grazed the side of his head and her knee dug into his thigh.

"Ouch." West grabbed her leg to hold her still. "Don't move."

"Oh, God, I'm sorry." She froze in place, saving him from certain injury.

"I'm not sure why you think you need to sneak away whenever you find yourself wrapped in my arms." He rolled to the side, taking her with him so they were lying face to face. "Why the panic?"

She wouldn't meet his gaze, so he tipped her head up with two fingers under her chin. She sucked in a deep breath before she raised her eyelids, locking her gaze on his. "I don't know what to do with you."

West laughed and waggled his eyebrows. "I can think of a few things."

Kelsey's lips twitched before turning upwards and West couldn't resist leaning over to plant a kiss on her sexy mouth. He expected her to pull back, to push him away. He never expected her to meet him halfway. Their mouths meshed, their lips clinging for long seconds before Kelsey slipped her tongue out and pressed against him, urging him to open. West wasn't about to deny this woman—or himself—anything. He let her in.

The kiss started slow. Not a frenzied dance of need, but a gentle waltz of two people who were comfortable with each other—who'd danced this dance before. He let Kelsey lead. Let her take them on the tempo of her choosing. His body—specifically his groin—might be screaming for him to dive deeper—go faster—but he knew she needed to be in control for now. He'd pushed her enough in the last few days and realized the best way to get what he wanted was to give Kels a turn at the reins. Let her come to him.

West tangled his fingers in her hair, his grip loose but firm enough for her to know he was there. He wanted her aware of who she was kissing. Wanted to be sure she wasn't thinking about her ex while her tongue was tangling with his. She moaned into his mouth and need rocketed through him—had him tightening all over including his grip on her hair, making him pull on the silky strands. Kelsey surprised him again by reacting to the slight tug in a way he never expected.

She clawed at his back, thrusting her hips against his while she drove her tongue deeper into his mouth. It was like he'd flipped a switch. One minute they were on a leisurely stroll down the path of seduction, the next they were at a flat-out run. Her hands were suddenly everywhere. In his hair. Sweeping down his back. Cupping his arse. The sweat pants he wore didn't deter her. With ease, Kelsey slipped her hand inside his pants, beneath his briefs, and wrapped her fingers around his straining erection.

West tore his mouth from hers. "Slow down," he panted.

"Don't want to." She squeezed him as she stroked up his length and his eyes crossed.

"Jesus."

Kelsey laughed as she set a mind-numbing rhythm. "Nope. Just me."

Before West could utter another word, Kelsey pushed him to his back and crawled over the top of him. Her face hovered over his, the blaze of desire burning in her eyes hot enough to incinerate any protest he might have. "Kels." He brushed his fingers down her cheek and cupped her jaw. He'd give her anything. Everything. "You do me in."

She smiled. "There is a certain part of your anatomy I plan on doing."

The smile on her lips turned downright devious as she moved down his body, her hand still working him. He'd have to be an idiot not to know where she was headed, and as much as he wanted to feel that mouth of hers wrapped around his cock, he had to stop her before she took him past the point of no return.

"Kelsey." West slid his hands under her arms and tugged her back up. When he had her face above his, he kissed her. He didn't let himself linger too long though. His hold on control was thin already. And there was still that hand wrapped around his dick. "We have to stop now. Before we can't."

"But I don't want to stop." She thrust her tongue between his lips before pulling back to nip at him with her teeth, while that torturous hand did its best to get him off. "I want to make you feel good. Want you to make *me* feel good. I don't want to feel sad anymore. Just for a little while, I want to forget. Make me forget."

What the fuck? She was sad? Wanted to forget?

This wasn't about wanting him. It was about finding oblivion from whatever had put that look in her eyes when she'd asked him to hold her. He wasn't about to let her use him like that. She'd regret it just as much as him after they were done. Grabbing her wrist, he pulled her hand out of his pants. In a second, he reversed their positions and pinned her beneath him. Cradling her face in his hands, he left her no choice but to look at him.

"Kelsey?"

~

AIR RUSHED from Kelsey's lungs as the world turned upside down. Blinking rapidly, her eyes focused on West now looming over her with storm-gray eyes.

Oh God.

What did she say? He'd wanted to stop. She'd told him she didn't. That she didn't want to feel sad—wanted to forget...

Oh God.

"Kels?"

She closed her eyes and took a deep breath, but neither action stopped the pinch of anxiety from squeezing her stomach —her chest.

"Talk to me." West stroked the side of her face, the caress soft like his voice, making her want to lean into him—lean *on* him.

Kelsey couldn't avoid answering no matter how much she wanted to. Opening her eyes she met West's gaze and tried to divert his attention. "If you don't want me, just say so."

He laughed and rocked his hips against hers. "Does that feel like I don't want you? Me wanting you isn't in question, it never has been."

She licked her lips and fought for control of her careening emotions. On one hand, she wanted to lose herself in the pleasure that West could give—the bliss that would obliterate anything else from her mind. On the other, she wanted to curl up in a ball and cry for all her ex husband and mother-in-law had lost in the face of Marjorie's illness. Kelsey didn't think West would appreciate the last sentiment. Not when they were tangled together in her bed. Not when he'd had such an angry reaction to her helping Bry in the first place. She needed to change the subject before she revealed what was weighing on her mind. "When did you get here? How'd you get in?"

West's hands tightened on her head. "Stop trying to change the subject. Tell me what the hell is going on. You don't go from trying to sneak away before I'm awake to offering to give me a blowjob in a matter of minutes."

Kelsey shook her head, her movements limited by West's hold.

"Don't." He dug his fingers into her scalp. "Stop shutting me out."

"I'm no—"

"You are." His voice and body vibrated with the frustration he didn't try to hide. "You didn't ring when you got home like you promised. I was worried, so I let myself in with your spare key. And I can see just by looking at you that I was right to be concerned. *Talk to me.*"

"I..." She couldn't dump her baggage on him. Her past was something she needed to deal with on her own. And until she did, whatever it was they were moving towards couldn't happen—*shouldn't* happen. "I'm sorry."

West's gaze bore into hers for long seconds before he pushed himself up and off her. "This isn't just about sex."

"I know."

He climbed off the bed. "Do you?" he asked as he glanced around the floor.

"Of course." Kelsey suddenly became aware of her lack of clothing—that she only had underwear on. Feeling vulnerable, she reached for the blanket. She couldn't remember getting undressed. What else was she forgetting?

"Then you need to let me in." West shoved his feet into his shoes. "Trust me with more than your body."

"I do."

"You think so? When I say I want more than just sex, I mean I want everything. The good *and* the bad. Until you can give me that we're not sleeping together."

Kelsey wanted to pretend she didn't know what West was talking about—wanted to go back to forgetting everything while wrapped in his arms. She knew she held a part of herself back. But she needed to in order to protect her heart from the one person who had the power to break it. He'd done it before, whether on purpose or not didn't matter. West had left her heart bruised and bleeding once, and there was no way she was going to risk it happening a second time.

The fact he picked up on her reluctance complicated things. Sleeping together had been a big mistake. One she'd almost repeated.

"You're right. We shouldn't have slept together. It won't happen again."

West laughed—the sound loud and sharp in the morning quiet. "Oh, it'll happen again. You can bet on it."

Before she could get a word out, he leaned over and pressed his mouth to hers. Hard and fast, he kissed her and then spun on his heel and left the room. Clutching the blanket against her chest, she sat in stunned silence until the front door slammed closed. Startled out of her stupor, Kelsey glanced at her alarm clock.

"Shit." She threw the covers off and bounded out of bed. If she didn't get in the shower now, she'd be late for her nine o'clock appointment at the community college.

Showered and dressed in record time, Kelsey detoured through the second bedroom she used as her office to grab the relevant files before heading out the door not fifteen minutes after West had left.

West.

What the hell was she going to do about him?

About *them*?

~

WEST TOSSED his keys and wallet on the counter as he made his way to the coffee machine. He needed a shot of caffeine. Actually, he needed something a lot stronger to deal with the drama surrounding Kelsey, but coffee was all he'd allow himself this early in the day.

She was shutting him out, and while he wasn't sure she meant to do it, she definitely knew she was holding back. He was convinced it had to do with Bry and his mother. Maybe their past had a bit to do with it too. Oh, who was he kidding, he didn't have a clue what was going through her head.

Sighing, he dropped a pod in the machine and hit the button. As soon as the coffee was done, he'd grab a quick shower and head in to work. There was no point hanging out here stressing about the latest red light Kelsey had put in his way.

His coffee had just finished pouring when his phone rang. He thought about ignoring it in case it was Kelsey, but he doubted she'd be ringing him after the way he'd walked out on her. Glancing at the screen, he saw Cassie's smiling face staring up at him. Figuring it was work related, West answered.

"Hey, Cassie. What's up?"

"Um, well, there's been a small incident in the kitchen here at Are You Game?"

West could hear commotion in the background. "What sort of incident?"

"There was a small fire."

"Did you burn another cake?" West chuckled. Last time Cassie had forgotten about a cake in the oven, it was because her boyfriend Luc had distracted her.

"Ah, no, it was a little bigger than that."

He suddenly registered the nuances in Cassie's tone and his protective instincts kicked in. "Are you okay?"

"Oh, yes. No one was hurt." He nearly didn't catch the next words she mumbled into the phone. "Well, no one except your kitchen."

"How bad?" If someone had burnt down his new kitchen he'd be in trouble. *They'd* be in trouble. Both Weston's Catering and Are You Game? had full calendars over the next few weeks. "Tell me it's at least usable."

Cassie's silence said it all, and West took a deep breath and tried to focus on the fact no one was hurt.

"Okay. What's the damage?" He was heading out the door, his coffee forgotten in the face of this disaster. And that's what it was. He'd have to source another kitchen and get the repairs on this one started ASAP. "Never mind. I'll be there in fifteen."

He took the back streets and made it to the Are You Game? building in thirteen minutes. Two fire engines and a police car filled the parking lot and blocked the driveway so West had to park half a block down. When he reached the property boundary, a policeman stopped him.

"Sorry, sir. You can't go in there."

"I'm one of the owners." It was a small lie. A technicality really, because he *did* own the kitchen that had apparently burnt down—if not the whole building—if all the fire personnel were an indication.

"Name?" the officer asked with a skeptical expression.

"West. Weston Mann." The delay had him clenching his hands in frustration.

The cop stepped away to speak into his radio, but West didn't have to wait for someone to confirm his identity because Cassie came out of the building and headed their way.

"West. God, I'm glad you're here. I had to send Jody home because I didn't want to risk the baby breathing anything toxic, even though the firemen say it's okay. And Dan's out on a job and can't get back for at least another hour, so other than Kerry it's just me here." Cassie threw her arms around him, her body trembling slightly.

He held her close before pushing her to arms length. "Are you sure you're okay? Who was in the kitchen when it went up?"

She shook her head. "No one."

"Then how'd the fire start?"

"Come inside and I'll explain." She turned and headed back the way she'd come, the cop making no protest when West followed her.

The second Cassie opened the outer door, West could smell the smoke. It was a mixture of melted plastic and burnt timber. He tried to remember what was on today's schedule but the stench had him waving a hand in front of his face and concentrating on not inhaling too deeply.

"Electrical," Cassie said as they headed across the warehouse floor.

"What?"

"They said the oven shorted out." Cassie pushed open the door to the kitchen and West's eyes and nose stung from the smoke hanging in the air in spite of how clear it appeared. "They're trying to pump the air out the back door. We need to keep this one closed as much as possible so the smoke doesn't seep into the rest of the building."

"Too late," West muttered as he moved farther into the room, his shoes sloshing through the water left behind by the sprinkler system.

He could see the blackened stove and surrounding cupboards. Well, what was left of them anyway. "Who's in charge?" he asked Cassie.

"Guy in the red hat talking to Kerry." She pointed across the room. "She's giving her version of what happened. I already gave mine."

"Shouldn't they do that somewhere else? The air in here can't be good for our lungs."

Cassie shrugged. "Most of the smoke has gone now."

It might seem as though the smoke was gone, but the sting in his nose and eyes told him the air was still contaminated and they really shouldn't be in here. West strode across the room to where Cassie's employee and the fireman stood. He stuck out his hand and introduced himself. "Hi. I'm West Mann. Owner of this kitchen."

"Oh, right. Ms. Moreland said you'd be arriving soon. Station Officer Rhodes." He shook West's hand before turning back to Kerry. "That should do it. I'll be in touch if I need anything else."

West turned to Cassie's employee. "Kerry, why don't you and Cassie head out front away from—?"

"Cassie!" Luc's voice boomed through the building.

"Uh oh," Kerry mumbled.

"Who's that?" Rhodes asked.

"That would be Cassie's boyfriend, Lucas Wilhelm," West answered just as Luc came barging through the door with the cop from out front hot on his tail.

West watched as Cassie quickly sprang into action pacifying both Luc and the cop in few words. He marveled at how well his pint-sized friend wrangled her six-foot-five boyfriend with the simple batting of her eyelashes. As the trio headed back through the door with Kerry following, West turned back to Officer Rhodes. "So can you tell me what happened?"

"It looks like a straightforward electrical fire. Ms. Moreland had switched the oven on and left the room while it heated. Unfortunately, there was an exposed wire in the wall behind the unit."

"Are you sure? This kitchen is only a year old."

"Doesn't matter how new something is, exposed wires are a fire hazard waiting to happen."

"How long before I can get a crew in to clean this up and start repairs?"

"Ms. Moreland has an electrician coming in to check the rest of the wiring for potential problems. The ovens have their own circuit so I'd say it'll be fine, but best to be safe than sorry. Then your insurance company will want to take a look."

"I guess it really doesn't matter does it? The kitchen is out of commission indefinitely."

"Afraid so."

West's gaze travelled the room and landed on the pantry door. He nodded in that direction. "Do you think any of the food in there is salvageable?"

"The door remained closed during the incident so anything in sealed airtight containers should be okay, but if it's covered under your insurance I'd ditch it just in case." Officer Rhodes shook his head. "You can't afford to poison people in your line of work."

West ran his hand over the back of his neck and squeezed. "Great. Just great." He really didn't need this drama in his life right now.

"If you'll excuse me, I need to check in with my men."

West stared at the disaster in front of him for a few more seconds before heading in the direction of the back door. He needed fresh air and a plan. The fresh air was easy. The plan, not so much. First, he had to find a substitute kitchen. And fast.

11

———

Kelsey hung up the phone and took a deep breath. Letting it out in a rush, she slumped back against the sofa in relief. As much as she wanted to be there for Bry and his mother, she was glad he'd called to tell her not to visit tonight. In the mood she was in, she couldn't have put on a cheerful face for Marjorie and the woman didn't need any more angst in her life.

Her phone buzzed in her hand, making her jump. Glancing at the screen, she saw Shaye had sent her a message.

OMG! Did you hear about West?

She hadn't spoken to or heard from West since he'd stormed out this morning, so Kelsey had no idea what Shaye was talking about. Instead of texting back, Kelsey called. The phone barely rang when her friend answered. Before Shaye could say a word Kelsey's questions were tumbling from her mouth.

"What about West? Did something happen to him? Is he all right? He was fine this morning." She sucked in a big breath.

"Whoa. Slow down there, speedy. First, his backup kitchen caught fire. Second, he wasn't there, so as far as I know he's fine and no one at Are You Game? was injured either. And third, and most interesting I might add, *when* this morning did you see him?"

"I, um, the Are You Game? kitchen? But it's barely a year old."

"Coop said something about an electrical fault. And nice diversion. When did you see West?"

Kelsey could hear the smile in Shaye's voice. She didn't miss her friend's mention of Coop and wondered what was going on with them, but she wanted to steer clear of any type of relationship talk so didn't ask. Instead, she went with Shaye's recent lack of employment as her next attempt at distraction. "How's the job hunting?"

"Oh, complete change of subject. Nice try, my friend, but not good enough. When and where did you see the delicious Mr. Mann this morning?"

A sigh left Kelsey's throat before she could stop it.

"Tut, tut, tut. None of that. Spill." Shaye could be like a dog with a bone.

Thinking fast, Kelsey said, "He came over to talk about my new role as his office manager." That was plausible. Shaye knew she'd taken the job with Weston's because Kelsey had tried to talk Shaye into taking it instead now that she was unemployed.

"Oh my God! Did you sleep with him?" Shaye squealed in her ear.

"What?" Kelsey choked—stumbled over a denial. She couldn't lie to Shaye. Her friend would know straight away if she did so she went for another deflection. "Why would you ask that?"

"Oh, I don't know. The major freak out on your part about whether West was all right. The fact you saw him this morning when I know he was at Are You Game? *before* nine. That's awfully early to be at your place, don't you think?"

"H-he was passing by." Kelsey knew they were the wrong choice of words the second they left her mouth.

Shaye laughed. A deep, rolling laugh that went on and on, and Kelsey knew if she didn't get off the phone now, their secret would be out, because Shaye would pepper her with question after question until Kelsey caved and spilled her guts. She wasn't ready to talk about her and West yet. Hell, she couldn't get things straight in her own head, how would she explain it to her best friend?

"Look. I've gotta go. There's someone at the door."

"I didn't hear your doorbell, but by all means, runaway. I'll get the truth out of you soon enough," Shaye warned.

"Talk later." Kelsey hung up before Shaye said another word and then tossed the phone to the other end of the sofa. She knew her friend wouldn't let the subject lie as is and fully expected to get the third degree the next time they talked.

The room was quiet. The only noise was the chaotic thoughts racing around inside Kelsey's head. A minefield of emotions verse reasons verse memories that continued to plague her. Nothing was any clearer than it had been this morning when West had walked out on her. She didn't know what to do or think...

Her phone buzzed, and when she glanced over, she wasn't surprised to see a message from Shaye. Putting it off wouldn't make the text go away, so she leaned over and grabbed the phone, tapping the little envelope icon as she straightened.

You should really REALLY think about the way you felt when you thought something had happened to West.

Kelsey didn't want to contemplate her stomach-squeezing reaction to Shaye's first text. She knew her friend was right though. Knew she needed to sort out what was going on with her and West. To say she was terrified was an understatement. The man had the power to destroy her, and he didn't even have a clue.

Regardless of her reluctance to see or talk to him, there was no denying the urge to check everything was okay—check *he* was okay. He might need help organizing repairs on the damaged kitchen. She could help him coordinate the clean up and refit. Or she could supervise the rebuild while he got on with the everyday necessities of running Weston's Catering.

Flimsy excuses be damned. She wouldn't rest easy until she knew West didn't need her. It only took her a second to call him, but when his phone rang out and diverted to voicemail, Kelsey's earlier panic returned tenfold. She jumped to her feet and was across the room grabbing her keys and purse from the hall table on her way out the door before she thought about it.

Traffic was brutal. Then again, she didn't expect anything less at this hour of the day. Kelsey navigated peak hour—why it was referred to as an hour when the snarl of Sydney traffic lasted for at least five was beyond her—with little patience and a good amount of swearing as she headed to Are You Game? She soon discovered the place was locked up tight. Next, she drove a few minutes down the road to Weston's. The car park was full, but a quick scan of the vehicles told her West's four-wheel drive wasn't one of them. Pulling out her phone, she tried calling him again. This time, he answered on the first ring.

"Hey." He sounded tired, worn out in a way she hadn't heard before.

"Where are you?" she asked, her panic causing her voice to wobble.

"At home. Why?"

"I heard what happened."

"The group grapevine's alive and well I see."

"Do you need me to do anything?"

"Kelsey, what I need from you you're not willing to give."

"I, um..." Brakes squealed and a car blasted its horn, making her yelp.

"Are you driving?" West asked.

"No. I'm parked outside of Weston's." Kelsey wasn't sure she wanted to admit to her frantic search, except now she didn't really have a choice. She'd already revealed her whereabouts. "I was looking for you. You didn't answer your phone when I called before. I was worried."

"Kels," he sighed her name.

She could picture him frowning and rubbing his forehead like he did when something frustrated him. Until now, she hadn't admitted to anything that might overstep the friend's line. Her actions certainly spoke for her, but verbally she'd remained mute, even denied and fought against their connection. She'd been fighting a losing battle. One she'd been waging with herself for what seemed like forever. "Can I come over?"

"Careful. I might get the wrong idea."

He was right. It was irrational in the face of everything she'd said and thought, but she had to see him. Although he sounded tired, Kelsey had no doubt he *was* okay. Only she still couldn't shake the need to see with her own eyes. "Please."

There was a long silence before he sighed heavily into the phone. "No."

"No?" Her voice came out a croak as her throat closed up tight and her heart thudded inside her chest.

"I can't do it. I've got a lot of work to do if I'm going to keep Weston's from losing business in the next few weeks. I don't have the energy to fight with you too."

"Fight? What do you mean fight?" They were fighting?

West laughed, but the sound failed to convey any joy, just the opposite, and Kelsey's stomach felt hollowed out.

"Then let me help keep Weston's on track," she all but pleaded.

"You will be. Monday morning in the office."

"But surely there's something I can do now."

"Go home, Kelsey. If I need you before Monday, I'll call."

"But—"

"Night. Drive safe." He hung up before she could argue further.

"Fuck." She tossed her phone on the passenger seat. It bounced off the cushion, hit the dash and dropped to the floor with a thump. Not unlike her heart. He'd rejected her. This was exactly the reason she should never have gotten involved with him again.

WEST SHOVED his fingers through his hair and hoped he was strong enough to stick to his guns and that Kelsey wouldn't ignore his refusal to see her. He'd almost given in. When she'd uttered *please* in that whispery tone she used when they were tangling the sheets, his body had let him know instantly that it approved of her coming over. If she turned up on his doorstep against his wishes...well, his mind's wishes, his cock was all for a visit from Kelsey. The damn thing was rock hard and ready to go just from hearing her voice.

But he had to ignore his libido if he wanted to reach his end goal

—Kelsey in his life on a permanent basis. And he wasn't referring to her role as his office manager. Getting her back into bed wouldn't be all that hard now that they'd fallen there. He knew neither of them could really fight their attraction after they'd spectacularly proven their chemistry was just as explosive as he remembered it being when they were teenagers.

He scrubbed a hand over his face and took a deep breath. There wasn't time to be rehashing the latest in the go-stop saga that was his and Kelsey's relationship. He'd brought home the schedules, list of venues and employee rosters for Are You Game? and Weston's. The kitchen he'd secured the use of was an hour away from Weston's, so he'd have to factor in the extra travel time for staff as well as delivery of product.

"Fuck." He had so much to do, and he wanted it done now. Wanted everything ironed out so his business would run smoothly. West pushed back his chair and headed for the kitchen and a cold beer. He'd allow himself one to take the edge off his crazy day. Maybe it would trick his blood pressure into thinking it was the weekend and he could relax. Every muscle was currently vying for the title of first to snap.

Lights flickered across the living room wall. Because of the position of his house on the block, the only way headlights could hit that particular wall would be if someone had pulled into his driveway. If he thought his body felt strung tight before, it was nothing compared to now. Detouring into the front room, he headed for the window. He stood off to the side in the hope of not being seen by whoever had come over. West shook his head. He didn't need to look to know who'd come calling.

Kelsey.

When West looked out the window, he saw her lights were switched off and he couldn't hear the engine and its irregular timing, but Kels hadn't gotten out yet. Her hands clenched the steering wheel at the very top, snug together, while her forehead rested on the back of them. West was conflicted. He didn't know whether to go out to her or stay where he was. He'd asked her not to come because he knew if he saw her he'd give in to his need to be with her and settle for whatever little scrap of herself she'd offer him.

Before he could make a decision either way, she moved. Jumping back out of view, he held his breath. She wouldn't see him, but now he couldn't see her either. He remained motionless for what felt like an eternity until an unusual ringing snapped him out of his frozen state. Glancing in the direction of the noise, West saw his phone vibrating on the dining room table. He quickly walked over to see what the hell it was buzzing for.

The phone was new and he was still getting used to the different ringtones and sounds it made. When he picked up the device, he discovered the reason for his confusion. Somebody was trying to video call him.

Kelsey.

West slid his thumb across the screen to accept. He debated what to say while the call connected. Her shadowed face appeared. Even in the dark, she took his breath. She was smoking hot, there was no denying that, but what was it about Kelsey that grabbed him by the balls—by the heart—and squeezed? He'd certainly seen prettier women—dated some even. None of them, in his opinion, held a candle to Kels.

"I'm sorry." Her murmured words snapped him out of his thoughts.

"For?"

"For not doing as you wanted."

"Which time?"

"I couldn't stay away. I'm in your driveway."

"I know." He sighed. There was no point lying. If he wanted her to be open and honest, he needed to do the same. "I saw your lights when you pulled up."

"I just wanted to see you're okay."

"You're seeing me now." Not that she'd actually made eye contact since the call had connected, which seemed impossible when her face and his filled their screens.

"I know...I just..."

"Just what?" West went back to the window and pushed the blind aside so he could see her sitting in her car. "What are you doing here? And don't rush to answer. Think about it for a minute."

He'd let her think on it while he went and unlocked the front door. He didn't try to disguise his movements. West wanted her to hear the lock disengage. The sound of her sucking in a deep breath echoed through the house, and he knew she didn't have any real idea —or was choosing to ignore it—about why she'd come. With everything he had, he wanted to go out there and get her. Pull her inside and tell her to look at him and tell him she didn't feel it. But he knew he couldn't.

She had to come to him.

"Kelsey?"

"I don't know."

"Yes, you do." He moved deeper into the house, away from the door—away from temptation. "You have to be brave enough."

"I'm sorry. So sorry."

"You keep saying that, but I have no idea what you're sorry for." West lowered himself onto his bed. He hadn't switched on the light, keeping himself in the dark deliberately.

"For everything. For not being enough. For Bry."

"You're more than enough."

"Then why did you never say anything? Why didn't you come after me?"

"Aw, Kels." He flopped back on the bed and stared into the darkness. "We were just kids. And I was stupid. So fucking stupid. By the time I pulled my head out of my ass you'd moved on."

"I never moved on." Her sharp gasp filled the room. "I didn't mean that. That's not what I meant to say."

West was on his feet and heading for the door. "You wouldn't have said it if there wasn't a kernel of truth in there." He was halfway to the front door when she stopped him.

"Don't come out! *Please.*"

He froze in place and dragged a deep breath in through his nose. Holding it, he counted to five and then let it out slowly. "Talk to me."

"You ignored me. I thought I'd done something wrong."

"Jesus—"

"No. Let me finish before you say anything."

"Okay." It was killing him not to have this conversation face to face. This stupid video call thing didn't count.

"You always made me feel too much. Good and bad. So when it went bad, it hurt so fucking much and I couldn't talk to anyone. We agreed we wouldn't. Then there was Bry. So easy. So simple. And he didn't make me feel so...open—so raw—when I looked at him. God." She sucked in a breath. "I promised I'd never let anyone hurt me like that again, West. *I promised.*"

"Come inside."

"No. I can't. Not now." She sniffed, and it killed him to know he'd done that to her. Again. "I should go."

"No. Just come in. No strings. It doesn't mean anything more than one friend comforting another."

"We're not friends. We crossed that bridge years ago."

He got what she was saying, but whether they were physically intimate or not didn't mean a fucking thing. She was still one of his closest friends, and he'd done the one thing he'd told himself he wouldn't. He'd hurt her.

Disregarding her instructions, he jogged out of the house and to her car before she realized he was coming. He flung her door open and reached in to unbuckle her belt, but she must have done it sometime after she'd arrived. With actions a little on the rough side, West pulled Kelsey from her car and wrapped his arms around her. She buried her head beneath his chin and slid her arms around his waist.

West couldn't say how long they stayed that way. How long she let him hold her close. How long she clung to him in return. But she finally pulled free of his embrace and took a step away, wiping her hands across her cheeks.

"I should go."

"I never meant to hurt you. Now or then."

Her gaze connected with his.

"I had no idea what I was doing. What I was walking away from."

He had to make her understand that he regretted what had happen between them. "I'd go back and fix it if I could."

Kelsey gave a nod but didn't say a word. She turned toward her car.

West followed her, moved closer. "We're not done."

She threw a half-smile his way. "I know. But I need to go."

"Call me when you get home. Let me know you're safe." He tucked a strand of hair behind her ear, lingered along her jawbone. "It was never that you weren't enough, Kels. You were always too much."

Neither of them said another word as she got back in her car and closed the door. He waited until she'd started the engine and backed out of the driveway before he raised his hand to wave. Then he waited until her taillights were just a memory in the night before he went back inside.

12

Kelsey sat trapped in the corner. On her left were Coop, Joe and Nick, the empty chair belonged to James, who'd gone to the bar for another round of drinks. Shaye, Mel and Nikki completed their group on her right. There was no way she could get out except under. And crawling on the floor just didn't seem dignified no matter how badly Kelsey wanted to leave. She had no doubt Shaye had planned it that way. Her friend hadn't wanted Kelsey to have an easy escape.

It had taken Shaye over an hour to nag her into coming, and Kelsey still wasn't sure why she'd agreed. She'd spent a sleepless night after her discussion with West, and she felt as though she'd taken to her insides with a grater. She was raw and bleeding and she couldn't work out why or how to make the feeling go away. The group talked around her and Kelsey nodded on occasion to appear as though she were listening and involved, only she wasn't. Not until Nick said her name and she was forced to pay attention.

"Hey, Kelsey, I hear you've taken on managing Weston's," Nick shouted over the others who were having an animated discussion about what heinous thing to do to Shaye's ex-boss.

Kelsey smiled and nodded as she lifted her glass to her mouth.

West was definitely a subject she wanted to talk about as little as possible.

"When are you two going to come out?" Mel asked.

"Out?" Kelsey arched one eyebrow.

"Yeah. It's not like you guys can keep it hidden now that you'll be working together every day," Nikki added.

Kelsey shook her head. "I don't get what you mean. Keep what hidden?"

"I'll translate," Coop said. "They're asking when you and West are going to admit that you're a couple."

Cold water filled the back of her nose as Kelsey choked on the mouthful she'd just swallowed. "What?" She coughed and reached for a napkin.

Shaye patted her back while a big smile stretched her lips. "There, there, sweetie."

"But I thought..." Nikki murmured.

"Oh, you're not wrong," Shaye said. "Kelsey's in denial though."

"How can you deny it?" Mel asked. "You're either with someone or you're not. For instance, you're not with Bry anymore because you got divorced."

Kelsey's gaze darted from one friend to another. They all stared at her with varying expressions—from curious to surprise to smug—the last being Shaye of course. She sent her so-called best friend a dirty look. "We're not together. I don't even know where you got the idea from."

"The sparks," Nikki said. Beside her, Mel nodded and Shaye just had a smug try-to-deny-it-now look on her face.

"You and West always did have chemistry." Joe shook his head. "Never could understand how you ended up with Bry when you and West could light up a room."

"Who and West?" James asked as he put a tray of drinks on their table. "What have I missed?"

"Nothing." Shaye poked a finger in Kelsey's ribs. "Kelsey is remaining mum on the subject of her and West."

"Kelsey and West? But aren't you getting back together with Bry?" James asked, his forehead wrinkling in confusion.

"What? No!" Kelsey had no idea where all this talk was coming from. No one but Shaye knew something was going on between her and West, and even she wasn't privy to any details. As for her and Bry...where would James get *that* from?

"You're getting back with Bry?" Coop leaned in close and lowered his voice. "Does West know?"

She turned to Coop and whispered, "There's nothing to know."

He studied her a few moments before nodding. "Good. I'd hate for you to make the same mistake twice."

Kelsey gasped.

Coop leaned closer, his lips right next to her ear. "We both know you never should have married Bry." He smiled as he pulled away but it did nothing to calm the unease churning in Kelsey's stomach.

Instead of questioning Coop further, Kelsey focused on James and what he'd said about Bry. She needed to squash that particular kind of gossip before it went any further. "James, why would you think I'm getting back with Bry?"

James took his seat and pushed the tray around the table for everyone to grab their glass. "I know someone who works at the home Mrs. Newman is in. She said you guys have been in there together a lot lately. Said she saw you cuddled up in the visitors lounge one morning."

"We weren't *cuddled up*. I was comforting him after a particularly bad time with his mother. She's not been well. I'd do the same for any of you." Kelsey waved her hand to encompass the group. She didn't want to go into detail about Marjorie's condition. From what Bry had told her, nobody knew how bad things had gotten with her health, and Kelsey didn't want to reveal too much of his personal information, but she also didn't want anyone getting the wrong idea about her and her ex.

James shrugged. "Guess that explains it."

Kelsey didn't think he sounded all that convinced, but before she could say any more, Zac arrived. She was startled by the venomous look he threw her way. If looks could kill, she'd be six feet under. What the hell had she done? He'd been acting strange at recent get-togethers, and there was the weird vibe she'd gotten from him last Friday, but this was the first time he'd shown her any real outright hostility.

Coop leaned his shoulder into hers. "Ignore him. He's being a prick lately."

She glanced at Zac's twin. "So I'm not imagining things?"

Coop laughed. "Hell, no. Watch this. I'll show you it's not just you he's got a problem with." He leaned over her to tap Shaye's cheek. "Hey, hot stuff. We still on for later?"

Shaye's smile and eyes were full of sexual innuendo as she moved closer to Coop, the two of them all but in Kelsey's lap now. "Think you can handle me?"

"Oh, I'll handle you all right." Coop's gaze dropped to ogle Shaye's cleavage.

"For fuck sake." Zac slammed his empty glass down on the table. "I'm not hanging around to watch this shit."

Kelsey watched him storm off. Mouths hung open all around the table. Obviously, she wasn't the only one shocked by Zac's behavior.

"See. Told ya." Coop winked as he sat back in his chair.

"Did you just do that to piss your brother off?" Shaye asked.

"Yep." A smug smile curled Coop's lips.

"Why you—"

"*Shaye,*" Coop murmured.

To Kelsey's surprise, Shaye sat back in her seat, mouth closed. Kelsey couldn't believe Coop could silence Shaye so quickly. She'd seen the head of steam her best friend was building up. Normally, it took a good rant for Shaye to let it go, but Coop had managed to do what Kelsey had thought impossible, and by only uttering her name.

"Ah, is there something going on between *you two* we don't know about?" Nikki asked, her gaze bouncing from Shaye to Coop and back again.

"Nope." Coop picked up his beer and grinned. "Not yet."

Kelsey was happy for the conversation to head in that direction.

She leaned back in her chair and let her friends debate the Shaye-and-Coop development while she contemplated the situation with West. Now that she'd revealed so much of her inner turmoil, she wasn't sure where they stood. She'd called him to let him know she'd arrived home safe. They'd spoken only a few words before hanging up, and neither had mentioned what had been said during their video call. Or after he'd come out of the house.

Her phone rang, snapping her to attention. Fear and excitement warred inside her. The possibility of West being on the other end of the call delivered conflicting emotions. Kelsey was worried their conversation had left both of them with a bad taste in their mouths. She certainly regretted revealing the depth of hurt he'd caused her in the past, but there wasn't anything she could do about it now.

She scrambled to get her phone out of her bag before the call switched over to voicemail. Caller ID showed it wasn't West but Bry on the other end, and Kelsey instantly got a bad feeling in her chest. "Bry?"

"Mum had a stroke," he choked out.

"Oh, God, Bry. I'm sorry."

"It's bad. Can you—"

"Yes, yes." She shoved her chair back and nudged Coop with her knee. "I'll come right now."

"Thank you, Kelsey. I don't know what to do."

Kelsey could hear the tears in Bry's voice and quickly shuffled past the guys to get out. "I'll be there as soon as I can."

"She's in North Shore Private. Where Dad was." His voice cracked, the last words were murmured in a desolate tone that squeezed Kelsey's heart.

She didn't know what to say. How to comfort him over the phone when there were no words that could make the situation better. "I'll be there soon." She hung up and dug in her bag for her keys.

"Problem?" James asked as she looked up at the group.

"Bry's mum has had a stroke. I have to go. I'll catch you all later."

"Let us know if he needs anything," Nick said.

"I will." She turned to leave but Coop grabbed her arm.

Turning back, she found Coop eyeing her with concern. "Let West know where you're going. Don't let him find out from one of us."

"Ah, okay." Kelsey wasn't sure why Coop thought West had a right to know where she was going, but as one of his best friends—and a close one of her own—she valued his advice and quickly tapped out a text as she rushed out of the pub to her car.

WEST DROPPED the phone in his lap as he watched Kelsey's car wiz past. He'd just parked when he received her text and reading the words sliced him up in a way he couldn't explain.

On way to Bry.

He figured something had happened with Bry's mother, but with so few words and no real meaning behind them, no one would blame him for thinking the worst. The jealousy and anger that filled him each time Kelsey dropped everything to go to Bry only left him feeling like a jerk. But he couldn't help his reactions even knowing the state of Bry's mother's health. West opened his door, but he didn't get out. Suddenly spending a few hours at the pub with his friends held no appeal.

Not without Kelsey.

He couldn't really afford the time away from work either. He'd spent the day sorting out the details for the next few weeks, but he had to be realistic and accept it was possible his second kitchen would be out of action for months. The insurance company wasn't sending anyone out until late next week, and until then he couldn't touch the charred mess. Reaching over, he grabbed the door and slammed it shut. A night at home surrounded by paperwork wasn't exactly the most riveting Friday evening, but West could think of only one thing more interesting, and that wasn't an option.

West started the car, but before he left he sent a text to Coop, letting him know he wouldn't be turning up. He'd reversed out of his spot and was pulling out of the parking lot into traffic when his friend called.

Activating the integrated phone system with the button on his steering wheel, West answered. "Hey."

"Is she really the only reason you were coming?" Coop asked.

"No. Yes." West checked over his shoulder before changing lanes. "I wasn't coming until you dropped your not-so-subtle hint that Shaye was dragging Kels out."

"You know where she is?"

"Yeah," he sighed. "Do you know what happened to Bry's mum?"

"Stroke."

"Ah, shit." West could totally understand why Kelsey had gone running off to Bry now.

"Yep. And from what James has just been telling us, it seems that good old Bry has been keeping mum about Mum," Coop said.

"Huh? What do you mean?"

"James knows some woman that works at the home where Mrs. Newman is. She told him that the junior Mrs. Newman has been there with her *husband* in recent days and that the senior Mrs. Newman is not doing well and hasn't been for a while."

"Why the hell would he keep that from us?" West asked as he turned off the main road onto a side street. The conversation was getting too distracting to be navigating through traffic at the same time. He spied a parking spot about fifty meters down and pulled into it.

"Well, I don't know about you, but I haven't seen Bry more than two times in the last few months. He's skipped our usual Friday drinks for weeks."

West thought about it for a moment. "You know, I don't think I've seen him in over a month." He'd heard him though. Loud and clear through Kelsey's phone. Twice.

"Wonder what's up with that? It's not like there's an issue between him and Kelsey that would be keeping him away. They've never had any issues."

"If what James said about Bry's mum is true, then her condition might be the reason."

"Okay, we've danced around it long enough and you completely ignored my husband comment. Are you okay with Kelsey running off to him?"

West sucked in a breath. "Why wouldn't I be?" If Coop knew something he didn't...

"So you know she's not just standing beside him?"

"What?" West had no idea what his friend was talking about, but he wanted details. Fast. "What the fuck does that mean?"

Coop sighed. "This friend of James said she saw them in each other's arms in the visitors lounge at the home."

Whoa. That he wasn't okay with. West's brain told him Kelsey would never be with Bry after being with him, but his heart was a whole other story. It ached along with his gut as acid churned in his stomach.

"I'm taking your silence to mean this is news to you."

"I'm sure there's a reasonable explanation." There had to be.

"Oh, there is. And for what it's worth, I believe her."

West waited but Coop didn't elaborate any further. "Well don't leave me in the dark, man."

"She said she was comforting him after a bad episode with his mother like she would any one of us."

"And you believed her?" He trusted Coop's judgment.

"Yeah. I also think Bry is taking advantage of Kelsey's generosity. She's always been the bleeding heart among our group."

"Yes, she has." West scrubbed his fingers back and forth on his forehead. "I get why he would though."

"Doesn't mean you have to like it," Coop said.

"Oh, I definitely don't like it, but what can I do about? I can't exactly tell her not to go."

"No. I guess not."

West closed his eyes and leaned his head back against the seat. For long moments, neither of them said a word, only the faint crackle of the open phone line filled the car. He should hang up and head home. "Listen, I gotta go. I'll talk to you later."

"Want me to come over?" Coop asked.

A bark of laughter left West's throat. "What? This little deep-and-meaningful isn't enough? Now you wanna come hold my hand too?"

Coop laughed. "Nah, I was actually thinking I wouldn't have to pay for my beer at your place."

"Ha! Think again. My fridge is still full of the case you brought round Monday night."

"Actually, Zac paid for that." Someone yelled Coop's name in the background. "Okay, I'm being summoned by a hot chick. I have a feeling this is going to be my lucky night."

"At least one of us is getting some," West murmured.

"What?"

"Nothing. Catch ya later."

"We still on for tomorrow? You want me to look at the kitchen, right?" Coop asked.

West had forgotten he'd asked his friend to give him an estimate on repairs. "How 'bout we leave it until next week. The insurance guy isn't coming until Thursday, and I can't touch it until after he's been and given his seal of approval for the claim to go through." Not that he needed the insurance money to pay for the damage, but he paid his premiums so he may as well get his money's worth.

"Call me when you know when."

"Will do." His phone beeped signally an incoming call. "Gotta go, someone's trying to call. It might be Kels."

Before Coop could say a word, West tapped the screen on his phone to drop their call and pick up the new one.

"Hello."

"West?"

"Kels? You okay?" She sounded anything but okay, and when he heard her sob he bolted upright in his seat. "What's wrong, baby? Where are you?"

Her sobs echoed through the car for long minutes and West felt powerless to help her. He couldn't even drive to her. He didn't have a clue where she was.

"S-she's gone."

"Tell me where you are and I'll be there."

"I. Bry. He's devastated." Never mind Bry, West could hear the devastation in *her* voice.

"Tell me where."

"I don't think. Hang on." Sound was muffled and West figured she must have covered the phone with her hand for a moment. "I have to go. I'll call you later."

"Kelsey! Don't you dare hang up without telling me where you are."

"I'll call you later. Promise."

"Dammit. Stop shutting me out." West slapped his palm on the steering wheel.

"I'm not. Bry's not in any condition to see anyone right now."

"What about you?" Who was going to support her through this?

"Later."

The connection cut off before West could get another word out. He slapped the wheel again. And again. Pain radiated up his arm, but he didn't care. Frustration and anger burned a hole in his gut and the throb in his hand and wrist gave him something to focus on other than Kelsey's latest mixed signals.

If she didn't want him, why had she called? And what the hell was he supposed to do—to think—when she reached for him and pushed him away at the same time?

13

Kelsey let the car roll to a stop at the kerb. She switched off the lights and engine and sat in the dark, staring through the passenger window at the house. There wasn't a light shining in any of the windows, causing her to second-guess her decision to come here for the millionth time. It was after one am, and West was obviously asleep. In the end, her need for comfort made her grab her purse and climb out of the car. The last few hours had been a hellish nightmare. Doctors and reports and a soul-sapping sorrow she'd never felt before. Marjorie might not have been her mother, but the woman had given Kelsey more maternal love than she'd received from anyone else in her life.

She stumbled on the uneven path as she made her way to the house, the streetlight didn't illuminate this far into the yard and without a porch light to guide her, Kelsey took extra care not to trip on the steps. But when she reached the door, she hesitated, turned around and stared at her car. What if he wasn't home? What if he was and wouldn't let her in? She'd never needed anything the way she needed West's arms wrapped around her right now. Eventually, the desperation to feel connected clawing at her insides won out over her fears and she spun back around and pressed the doorbell.

The bell echoed on the other side of the closed door and she held her breath until she heard footsteps rushing over timber floors. When the door opened to reveal West in nothing but a pair of low-slung boxer briefs, Kelsey didn't know if it was exhaustion, grief or the naked masculine perfection in front of her that rendered her speechless.

Thankfully, West didn't need words to know what she wanted. What she needed. He reached out and grabbed her hand. Pulling her inside, he closed the door before wrapping his arms around her and holding her close. She gave in then. Let her purse drop to the floor at their feet and her tears fall to his chest. Kelsey had no idea how long they stood there. How long the wretched sobs racked her body. But when West slipped an arm behind her knees and lifted her up to cradle her against him, she was relieved—grateful that he was taking care of her when there was no way she could.

Without a word, he walked through the house to his room. Kelsey clung to his neck when he lowered her to the bed and tried to pull away. "No."

"I'm not going anywhere." He brushed his fingers down her cheek. "I just want to get you something more comfortable to sleep in."

She let her arms slip from around him and fall to her sides. "I should go home." Her protest was weak. She didn't have the strength to walk out to her car never mind the desire.

"You wouldn't have turned up on my doorstep at this hour if you wanted to go home," West said as he pulled the second drawer on his dresser out and grabbed a shirt. He came back to the bed and held out his hand. "C'mon, let's get you out of those clothes. Do you want a shower?"

For a split second, she thought about it. Thought about trying to wash away the smell of death that seemed to be clinging to her, but with her eyelids drooping and her arms and legs feeling as though they were weighted down with lead, Kelsey figured she'd end up in an exhausted pile at the bottom of the shower if she tried. "No."

"Okay. Straight to bed it is."

West undressed her with a minimum of fuss, and before Kelsey could come up with another feeble argument about going home, she found herself surrounded by the softest T-shirt she'd ever touched. He helped her beneath the covers before crawling into the bed on the other side. Kelsey wasn't sure what she expected, but it wasn't for West to pull her against him, his chest to her back, and just hold her. His comfy shirt wasn't the only thing she found herself enveloped in.

His warmth seeped through her skin to heat the cold that had settled in her chest since she'd arrived at the hospital to discover she was too late. He didn't ask questions—didn't press for any details—and Kelsey was so grateful to not have to relive those horrible moments if only for the rest of tonight.

She focused on his steady breathing, the beat of his heart against her spine. With each puff of air, each pulse of blood, she sank deeper and deeper into exhaustion, knowing that everything would be okay because West had her.

WEST WAS PRETTY sure he should be nominated for sainthood. He'd been lying here with an almost-naked Kelsey in his arms, her curvy ass snuggled up to his groin, for hours. And for hours, he'd had a hard-on he could do nothing with. Then again, a saint wouldn't think about sex at a time like this, half-naked woman or not. Self-recriminations for being such a deviant when Kels was clearly hurting bounced around his brain. She'd lost someone close—someone she cared about deeply—and his body wanted to roll her over so he could bury his cock inside her. Damn, he was such a selfish prick.

He glanced over at the alarm clock. Seven nineteen. The sun hadn't been up an hour yet, and with his room being on the south-west side of the house, it was still fairly dark. Hopefully, Kelsey would get a few more hours sleep before she was forced to face reality again. Pulling his arm out from under her, West eased away slowly so he wouldn't disturb her. She murmured something he didn't catch before rolling over and cuddling into the quilt. Satisfied she wasn't going to wake, he got out of bed and headed for the bathroom and a desperately needed cold shower.

Cold showers on winter mornings were not good. West shivered his way through, but at least he managed to get his hard-on under control, if not eradicated completely. The fact he had the woman of his dreams in his bed couldn't be ignored entirely. Slipping into jeans and a T-shirt, he headed for the kitchen and coffee. He checked Kelsey was still sleeping on the way and found her in the same position he'd left her. There was no denying the thrill that coursed through him at the sight of her in his bed. He'd waited years to get her there. Unfortunately, the circumstances weren't what he'd expected.

It had to be a good sign that she'd come to him in the middle of the night. She could have gone to Shaye, or even stayed with Bry, but instead she'd driven here. To him. That said a hell of a lot about the way she felt. Now, if he could only get her to be honest about those feelings when she wasn't in the pit of grief. West didn't delude himself though. He wasn't taking her arrival on his doorstep in the dead of night as a confession of anything. If she performed to her usual standard, she'd be denying and backpedalling and throwing up those damn red lights the second she woke.

With a sigh, West left the room and made his way down the hall. He spotted her bag on the floor by the door. She must have dropped it when he'd pulled her inside. West walked over, scooped it up and took it into the kitchen with him. He placed it on the counter next to his keys and wallet. Seeing Kelsey's bag—her personal belongings— beside his pulled him up short, and he stared at them. Wished it was something he saw every day.

He reached out to brush his fingers over the leather strap when her phone rang. For a second, he froze, but when the shrill ring blasted through the room again, he opened her bag and searched for the phone. When he saw who it was, it took him a heartbeat to decide whether or not to answer. Bry.

Taking a deep breath, West hit answer and brought the phone to his ear.

"Kelsey. I'm sorry to call so early after last night."

"It's West. Kels is still asleep." West might resent this man for a few things, but he did the polite thing and offered his condolences. "Sorry to hear about your mum."

"Oh. Um, thanks."

Silence filled the line, and again West was forced to do the right thing when all he really wanted to do was hang up on the guy. He was sure Bry only wanted to impose on Kelsey's soft heart again. "Can I help you with something?"

"Um, no, I just wanted to let Kelsey know our appointment at the funeral home is at eleven today."

"*Our* appointment?"

"Yeah, Kelsey said she'd come with me when I pick out Mum's coffin," Bry's voice broke over that last word.

And right there West felt like the biggest bastard on the planet. "I'll let her know. Does she have the address?" he asked.

"I was going to come pick her up."

"Oh, right. I'll let her know what time to be ready then. Do you need help with anything else?" It pained him to ask, but he had to. Had to forget this man had a connection to Kelsey that West envied— wanted to sever. One he wanted for himself.

"No. I can't do anything else until all the paperwork is dealt with. One step at a time. Funeral planning today." West heard Bry suck in a deep breath and let it out in a rush. "To be honest, I can't cope with thinking about more than that right now."

"I can understand that. Hang in there, and you know how to get me if you need anything. Same goes for the rest of the gang. We're all here for you." West wanted to be sure Bry knew Kelsey wasn't the only one he could call on. Maybe then he wouldn't demand so much from her. "Any time. Day or night."

"Thanks. I appreciate it."

"I'll make sure Kels is home and ready in time for you to pick her up." West couldn't stop himself from implying she wasn't there now. He hadn't outright said she was at his house, but Bry would have to be stupid not to get the hint, and he definitely wasn't.

"Oh, I can pick her up from...wherever."

West smiled. No, definitely not stupid. "Nah, that's fine, she'll want to change out of yesterday's clothes anyway."

"Ah, right. Okay. Tell her I'll be there around ten-thirty to pick her up."

"Will do."

"Thanks." Bry paused but West didn't fill the silence. "Bye then."

"See ya, Bry. And don't forget. Anything you need. Any time."

"Yeah, okay. Thanks."

West waited for Bry to hang up before pulling Kelsey's phone away from his ear. He took note of the time and decided he'd make omelets for breakfast. There was no way Kels would let him go with her to help Bry, so he'd make sure she knew he was there for her in other ways. Ensuring she got sleep and ate properly would do for now.

Kelsey rolled over and stared at the unfamiliar ceiling. It took her a few seconds to remember where she was, but when she did, she was slammed with two things. Grief and guilt. The grief she could easily explain. Marjorie was dead. She might not have seen the woman in recent months, but for years their contact had been daily. The guilt came from a number of reasons. There were so many things she'd done she regretted—was ashamed of. Her biggest shame surrounded her.

She'd taken advantage of West by coming here.

He'd welcomed her unconditionally and she felt sick to the stomach when she thought about the way she'd treated him. She'd let him in only to shut him out then let him in again. Except she'd never let him get too close. And yet when she'd needed him, she hadn't thought about what that would do to their complex relationship. She couldn't deny it any longer. There was something between them. Something that, even now, when she couldn't hide from it any longer, she didn't want to examine.

She could hear him at the other end of the house. He was in the kitchen, and if the aromas seeping into the room were a clue, he was cooking. Kelsey knew West cooked for the enjoyment of it, but also because he liked to feed people, her in particular. She'd lost count of the number of meals he'd turned up on her doorstep with over the last three years. Ever since she'd separated from Bry, she'd had the pleasure of eating one of West's meals each week.

Since she'd separated from Bry...

Oh God. She'd never thought about it before. But that was when West had started feeding her. He'd been the first to arrive bearing a housewarming gift to that tiny apartment she'd rented the first year. Then he'd helped her find her house, helped her fill it with used furniture and even showed her how to change fuses when she hadn't had a clue where to find them never mind replace them.

Had he been leading up to this? To them getting together? The more she thought about it, the more she remembered all the little things he did for her—little things that straddled the *friend's* line—the more she was convinced that West had been waging a slow campaign of seduction. She'd been blind. Stupid. Hurtful. Thoughtless. Without knowing it, she'd taken advantage of him. Except last night she'd known. All those second thoughts about coming over...

"Hey, sleepy head. Hungry?"

Jolted from her thoughts, Kelsey's gaze darted to the doorway where West leaned against the frame. He wore a snug dark-blue T-shirt and jeans so faded they were white in places. All the right places. "Um, I guess." Her stomach was hollow and she figured she could probably eat a horse if it was the only thing on offer, but after what she'd been thinking before he showed up, Kelsey wondered if it might be best to get out of here as quickly as possible.

"C'mon then. Up you get." He pushed off the wall and strolled towards her. "I've made omelets. And bacon."

Bacon. Her weakness.

He held out his hand and Kelsey did the only thing she could. She slid her hand into his and let him pull her off the bed and to her feet. "I should get dressed..." She glanced around for her clothes.

"Nah, the shirt covers you and you've only got yesterday's clothes to put on."

She looked down. West was right. The hem brushed her lower thighs and the sleeves hit her elbows.

"Do you want coffee or tea with breakfast?"

Kelsey let him lead her from the room. "Coffee. I need the caffeine hit."

"You also need food. Did you eat dinner last night?" he asked as he ushered her into a chair at the table.

"A sandwich from the hospital cafeteria." She didn't add that it had been midnight when she'd gulped it down.

He exaggerated a shudder and pretended to gag, making her smile. "That's not food. In fact, I'm pretty sure they only serve nuclear waste in those places."

She laughed. "It wasn't that bad." The bread was a bit hard and the lettuce a little brown on the edges, but it had served its purpose and filled a hole.

"Well, this feast will be a definite improvement on your last meal." He disappeared into the kitchen only to return moments later with a tray loaded with their breakfast.

"Oh my God. How much food did you cook?" Kelsey eyed each plate as he set it in the middle of the table. There was a huge pile of bacon stacked on one and the biggest omelet she'd even seen on another.

West shrugged as he handed her an empty plate. "I'll have the leftovers for lunch."

"And dinner, I think." She picked up a piece of crispy bacon and popped it into her mouth.

"Hey, I had my eye on that bit." He mock frowned at her.

Kelsey grinned as she chewed. It was perfectly crisp with just enough bacon grease to satisfy the sinful indulgence without clogging the arteries. Typical of West to try and make an unhealthy treat healthy—not that she cared either way. Bacon was bacon, and she'd eat it until there wasn't a slice left if she could.

"How much omelet do you want?" He held a knife in the middle of the egg-covered plate. "Half?"

"No. A quarter. That way I'll have room for more bacon." She grinned and reached for a second piece.

"A third." He didn't wait for her to agree. And before she could protest, he was putting a good chunk of the fluffy omelet on her plate.

"*West.*"

"*Kelsey.*" He mimicked her tone.

"I won't be able to eat all that."

"Fine. Don't finish it." He put the rest of the eggs on his own plate. "Serve yourself some bacon while I go get the coffee."

She did as she was told. Of course, she picked through the plate to find the crispiest pieces. By the time West put a mug in front of her, Kelsey had polished off another two slices and started on her eggs.

"Good?" he asked as he took his seat.

Kelsey covered her mouth with her hand and spoke around a mouthful of fluffy eggs. "You have to ask?"

He grinned and then scooped a forkful of omelet into his mouth.

Neither of them spoke for the next few minutes. It took no time for Kelsey to finish everything on her plate, and she stared at the empty surface with confusion. She would have sworn she wasn't that hungry when West served her that huge piece of omelet.

"You want more?" He indicated the few strips of bacon still on the plate between them.

Kelsey shook her head. "No. I'm good. Surprised I managed to finish what you served me actually." Then again, it was bacon...

"More hungry than you thought then." West picked up his mug and took a sip.

"Must have been," she said while eyeing those last couple of pieces.

West laughed. "Go on. You know you want to."

She looked up to find him grinning at her. Smiling sheepishly, Kelsey reached over and snatched up the remaining bacon and dropped it on her plate.

"There you go. Not so hard, was it?" he asked.

"No. What'll be hard is the extra exercise I'll have to do to get rid of the fat these things are going to lay on my butt and thighs."

He put his mug down hard on the table, making everything rattle, and leaned forward. "First, you don't exercise on the best of days. Second, there's nothing wrong with your butt or your thighs. They're both perfectly sized and shaped, and I love running my hands over them."

Kelsey's pulse raced. Heat flooded her core and a tremor rippled through her. "I, um..."

West leaned back and picked up his coffee. He appeared calm. Except those penetrating grey eyes. His eyes were a firestorm of need and want and hunger, and Kelsey's body reacted to the blatant desire he aimed her way. She tightened—like one of those vacuum bags she stored her winter clothes in—shrinking until nothing but her bone-deep yearning for him showed.

It all came down to this. The all-consuming attraction she had for him. Now that she'd slept with him again, the walls she'd erected all those years ago were crumbling.

Crumbling quicker than she could deal with.

Quicker than she could patch them up.

"Finish your breakfast, Kels."

Instead of answering, she dug into another slice of bacon. The longer she could avoid examining her true feelings the better, because she wasn't ready for where this was going—where they were going. Wasn't ready to put her heart on the line again. She was popping the final bit of bacon in her mouth when West spoke.

"Bry phoned while you were still asleep."

Kelsey had to swallow carefully so she didn't choke at his words. "What?" Kelsey sat up straight, the bacon hitting her stomach like lead. "Bry rang here?"

"No. He called your cell."

"Oh." She pushed back her chair. "I should call him back."

"No need. He just wanted to let you know he'd pick you up at ten-thirty to go to the funeral home."

"You answered my phone?" Kelsey wasn't sure how she felt about that. Too many emotions were churning around inside her. Concern over what West might have said to her ex-husband about where she was definitely led the charge though.

West nodded. "I wasn't about to let it continue to ring and wake you up. You needed to rest."

"Oh." Kelsey didn't know what to say. Bry would have been surprised when West answered her phone, but hopefully the distress over his mother's passing would numb him to the strangeness of it. As far as she knew, the two men hadn't had any contact since her and West had fallen into bed together. She knew West wasn't comfortable with her supporting Bry as much as she did, and she hoped he hadn't said anything about it.

She also hoped he hadn't given away the fact she hadn't gone home last night.

14

———————

Kelsey was dreading the next few hours. It had been an exhausting couple of days. Ones where she hadn't dared talk to West for fear she'd crumble completely. She had to be strong for Bry. As much as she knew it wasn't really her place to support him so fully, she also knew the man was falling apart. Without her to drive him around and help start the process of straightening out his mother's estate, he would still be standing in that hospital corridor where she'd found him the night Marjorie died.

Today was the funeral. And even though she knew she shouldn't go with Bry, she hadn't been able to refuse him when he'd asked. He'd looked so lost—so gutted—that every one of her heart's strings had pulled tight and threatened to cut off her blood flow. She'd been the one to notify all Marjorie's relatives and friends of her passing. To notify everyone of the time and place the service would take place. Bry couldn't even manage to shower, never mind coordinate a funeral.

The doorbell rang and Kelsey's stomach cramped. She hadn't eaten much in the last few days. She'd found a meal in her fridge with a note from West stuck to it each night, but other than that, they'd only had a handful of texts in the way of contact. He'd offered to come over every day since she'd left his house on Saturday, but Kelsey hadn't had the time or the energy to think about what was happening between them, and until she did she couldn't bring herself to lean on him. Not again.

Not if she was going to put a stop to whatever it was they were doing. And she had to. She didn't think she could risk her heart to him a second time, and it wasn't fair to either of them—but especially West—to continue seeing him unless she did.

With a sigh, she walked to the front door and opened it to find a pale and gaunt Bry standing on her front step. He really was a mess. He'd never get through today without her to guide him.

"The car is here," he said in way of greeting.

She glanced over his shoulder to see the funeral-home car waiting at the kerb. Taking a deep breath, Kelsey reached for the door to close it behind her. "I'm ready."

Bry held out his hand and then must have thought better of it, because he waved it in the direction of the street and the waiting car. "After you."

Kelsey smiled—more a grimace really—and moved past him. Leading the way, she glanced back to check he was following. She'd sent him home two hours ago to get ready and wait for the car. It was the first break, other than when she was asleep, that she'd had since he'd picked her up last Saturday to help chose his mother's coffin. He'd begged to sleep on her couch, and as usual, Kelsey found it impossible to refuse someone in need. They'd made a stop each day at his house for clean clothes, but other than that, Bry was basically living with her again. At least someone was benefiting from West's generous delivery of food.

Kelsey nodded at the driver when he opened the door for her. She climbed in and slid across the seat to make room for Bry. They'd be arriving at the church in about twenty minutes. One thousand two hundred seconds to brace herself for everyone's reaction. She was dreading it more than the funeral itself. Bry sat next to her and closed the door, but instead of offering him a reassuring smile like she'd been doing all week, she stared out the window and tried to focus on the passing houses.

They pulled up in front of the church all too soon, and Kelsey kept her gaze lowered as she got out of the car. She didn't want to face West or any of their friends just yet. Instead, she let Bry usher her inside to the pew reserved for immediate family and took a seat. There was no need for her to turn around, no need for her to make eye contact with anyone. She could feel more than one set of eyes on her. Their curiosity was understandable. It was the anger and confusion she was sure West would be feeling that she didn't want to see.

The service was simple—quick. Bry hadn't wanted anyone to speak, just the priest, and it didn't matter how much Kelsey had tried to convince him otherwise, he hadn't budged on that. Funny how he couldn't seem to make a decision about anything else but that he'd known with certainty. There were no pallbearers, only men from the funeral home dressed in black suits. Kelsey waited while the priest offered his condolences to Bry before they made their way out of the church behind the coffin.

She stood to the side and watched as the men loaded Marjorie in the back of the hearse for her final journey. Bry hadn't wanted a graveside service, instead opting for his mother to be lowered into the ground next to his father in private. He wouldn't even be there. He moved closer to her and despite her attempts to keep her distance as everyone came past to offer their sympathy, Bry kept including her in the conversations, kept pulling her closer.

Their friends waited until all other attendees had spoken to Bry before coming over. As much as Kelsey didn't want to look, her eyes sought West. She wasn't sure what it was swirling in those stormy-grey eyes, but she couldn't stop the catch in her breath nor the tears flooding her eyes and blurring her vision. She'd known seeing him would make her crack. Known the emotions she'd been holding at bay would come crashing down on her.

He stepped forward and pulled her into his arms, but she couldn't let him give her comfort. Not when she wouldn't be able to let go if he held her longer than a few seconds. She slipped from his embrace, avoided the eyes she knew would be filled with confusion and hurt, and turned to face the next of their friends. It seemed to take forever for the last person to come forward, for everyone to begin to move away and the driver of the funeral car to usher them back into the vehicle.

Kelsey slumped back against the seat and prayed she wouldn't lose it until after she got home. Until after she was alone and could let everything she'd bottled up run free. Bry didn't speak, and for that she was grateful. But her relief was short lived. When the car pulled up at her house and he exited with her, she knew she wouldn't be able to let go anytime soon.

WEST THREW his keys across the counter and made a B-line for the fridge. He yanked open the door, pulled out a beer and cracked the top. But when he brought the cold bottle to his lips, he couldn't drink. His frustration and anger were a boiling, seething mass inside him, and he had to let it out. The only way to do that was to confront the person who'd caused it.

Kelsey.

God it had ripped him up inside to see her looking so exhausted. And thin. He didn't know if anyone else would notice but he could tell she'd lost a couple of kilos since he'd held her while she slept Friday night. Had it only been five days ago that she'd left his house after spending the night in his arms? He'd lost track of the days, what with Weston's being so busy and his worry over Kels, he didn't know what day it was.

Standing there, watching Bry be totally oblivious to Kelsey's pain and need had solidified something for West. If he couldn't have her completely, couldn't be the one to support her, he had to walk away.

And by walk away he meant she couldn't work for him in any capacity. He'd have to find someone else to manage the books and his taxes. There was no way he could settle for the crumbs she'd been tossing his way.

Not anymore.

As he put the beer on the counter, he reached over and scooped up his keys. He slammed the front door on his way out. The small amount of satisfaction did little to appease his growing annoyance. West figured he was about to explode, and Kelsey was going to take the brunt of it. His fury may be an overreaction, but today had been the straw that broke the camel's back so to speak. He'd had enough of her pushing him away only to pull him close when it suited her and then push him away again.

He didn't remember the drive over. Couldn't say if he'd stuck to the speed limit or ran any red lights. His complete focus was on the coming confrontation with Kelsey. Slamming out of his car, West stopped to suck in a deep breath in an attempt to cool his jets some before he stormed into her house. With a little more control over his anger, he made his way up the path.

West thought about using his key but decided he better not. He should at least give her the courtesy of knocking, except when he reached the door, he found it open and Kelsey standing in the hallway with an armload of clothes. Men's clothes.

"What the fuck?" West didn't know he was going to open his mouth until his voice echoed off the walls.

"West? What are you doing here?" Kelsey's forehead creased and she looked over her shoulder.

"We have to talk," he said.

She turned to face him once more. "This isn't a good time."

"It's never a good time." He stepped closer, deeper into the house. "I'm tired of waiting for the *good time*, Kels."

"Please." She looked over her shoulder down the hall again before bringing her gaze back to his and then dropping it to stare at his chest. "Not now."

West had a feeling he knew why she kept glancing that way. He nodded towards the pile of clothes in her arms. "Want to explain that?"

She wasn't looking at him, so he doubted she saw his gesture, but she would have to be clueless not to know what he was talking about. "I...um..." Her struggled to find words didn't surprise him.

For the first time since he'd gotten there, West took his eyes off Kelsey and looked around. From where he stood, he could see into the living room. It was obvious she'd had company—still had company if he took into account the pair of men's dress shoes next to the coffee table. He'd seen hints of it this past week when he'd dropped off a meal each day, but he'd ignored it. He couldn't ignore it now. It was blatantly obvious Bry was staying with her.

"It's not what you think," she murmured.

He bought his gaze back to her. "You have no idea what I think or why I think it. You're too busy pretending nothing is going on and burying yourself in someone else's problems so you can avoid your own."

"That's not true," she argued.

"Isn't it?" He scrubbed his hand across his forehead.

"No. I'm helping a friend. Just as I would any other."

"Seriously?" West's mouth hung open. Did she actually believe that load of BS? "So you'd let any other *guy* friend stay over. Do his washing?"

"Bry's mother just died, West. What else am I supposed to do?"

"Support him without shutting out the man in your life for a start."

"The man in my life?" Kelsey lowered her voice. "We slept together once. It was a mistake."

He wasn't about to argue the number of times they'd slept together. They could pick that particular debate apart for hours. "Was it a mistake when you turned up on my doorstep in the middle of the night needing comfort too?"

"I—"

"Don't delude yourself. We're seeing each other. You wouldn't have had sex with me if you didn't feel something for me. And you wouldn't have knocked on my door after midnight just so I could hold you if you didn't feel it deeply. Stop lying to both of us."

"I can't deal with this now."

"Dammit, this has to stop!"

"What?"

"You shutting me out. Sneaking around behind closed doors like we're some fucking dirty little secret. Everything being on your terms."

"That's not—"

"Isn't it?" He stepped closer and she took a half-step back. "Who knows?"

"K-knows?"

"Yes. Who the hell knows we're seeing each other. And don't you dare fucking say we're not again. Do you have any idea how hard it was to watch Bry put his hands on you today? How hard it was not to give you the comfort I could see you needed? Any idea how much I wanted to pull you against me to hold you close—to claim your mouth in a kiss that would leave you with no doubt I'm here for you —leave no one in any doubt we're together?"

"I..." She shook her head.

"I know I fucked up before. But I'm not that boy any more. I know what I want. *Who* I want. And I know I have a lot to make up for, but I'm ready to do that and more, Kelsey. I just need you to meet me halfway."

"West," she whispered his name, her eyes glistening with tears, still shaking her head back and forth.

"Fuck." West couldn't do it. Couldn't stand here and argue with her when he knew full well she wasn't going to admit to a damn thing. Wasn't going to let him in and give him what he wanted. "I've had enough. I can't take it anymore. You either want to be with me or you don't. I can't keep doing this stop-start thing or continue to pretend I'm not so far gone on you that I can't see straight."

❀

Kelsey didn't know what to say. Couldn't think beyond the hurt, devastated look in West's stormy-gray eyes.

"Just as I thought." He dragged his hands through his hair. "I'm done pushing this. Done fighting for us on my own. When you're ready to be with me, *really* be together, out in the open for anyone to see, you know where to find me."

He spun around and stormed from the house. The slam of the door made her flinch, but other than that she didn't move. It wasn't until several minutes later that what had happened sank in.

"Oh God." He'd left.

"Kelsey?"

She turned to find Bry standing behind her. "Bry. I…"

"I should go," he said.

Oh God. Her cheeks filled with heat. He'd heard their argument. "I'm sorry."

Bry smiled. "You don't have anything to be sorry about."

"I do. You've just lost your mother. You need somewhere to recoup. Not somewhere with people arguing—"

"You should go after him."

"What?" She stared at her ex-husband.

"Go find him and fix it."

"I…it's not—"

He smiled. "Yeah, it is." Bry took a step closer.

Kelsey swallowed and confessed what was weighing on her heart before her mind could stop her tongue from forming the words. "I'm so, so sorry. I never loved you like I should have. Like you deserved."

He laughed and pulled her into a hug, the armload of his dirty clothes trapped between them. "We're both guilty of that."

She shook her head. "No. I—"

"Nope." He gave her a squeeze before letting her go. "No apologies necessary. We loved each other, still do, but it's not the kind of love you build a life on. And if we hadn't both been so intent on having that happy ever after, we might have worked out sooner that it was false walls we were putting up."

"Might have been better if we didn't like each other so much too." She gave him a tight smile. "I still feel guilty about all I cheated you out of."

Bry placed his hands on her shoulders and looked her right in the eyes. "I know what you can do to make it up to me."

Kelsey eyed him warily. "What?"

"Stop punishing yourself and West, and go after what *you* deserve."

Her eyes widened, her mouth dropping open, but before she could gain her wits, he was talking again.

"I've always known how you two feel about each other. And it shames me to admit part of my motive to get married was to stake a bigger claim on you than him." Bry smiled, but sadness and regret burned in his eyes. "So you see we both have things we're guilty of. Sorry for."

Kelsey stared at the man she'd married. He had been and always would be her friend, and yet she'd had no clue that he'd known about her feelings for West or that he'd felt threatened by them. "I don't know what to say."

"Tell me you're going to go find him. Tell me you're going to go fight for what you deserve. 'Cause you deserve a man who loves you to distraction and that man was never me. Would never have been me. West, on the other hand, he's that guy."

Her eyes and nose stung with the tears she held at bay.

"None of that." He tapped her on the end of her nose. "No tears. Not while I'm here."

Kelsey didn't argue when he took the pile of clothes from her arms. Or when he went into the living room and slipped his feet into his shoes. She still hadn't said a word when he came to stand in front of her again.

"Thank you, for going above and beyond." Bry leaned over and kissed her forehead. "You're more than I ever deserved, Kelsey."

With those parting words, Bry let himself out the front door and closed it quietly behind him. For a split second, she thought about going after him to offer him a lift. But the man was perfectly capable of calling a cab or flagging one down.

Bry was right. She'd gone above and beyond for him in the last few days.

Was West right though? Had she sunk herself into helping Bry so she didn't have to think about what was happening between them?

15

Kelsey had wanted to go after West on Thursday night, but she knew she had to be sure. If they were going to do this —if she was going to put her heart on the line again, she had to be one hundred percent certain it was what she wanted. So she'd taken a couple of days to think about it. *Really* think about it. She'd discovered some things about herself she wasn't proud of in the two days since he'd given her the ultimatum. He'd been right to call her on her behavior. She was ashamed to admit she probably would have continued to treat him the same neglectful way if he hadn't.

Once she'd decided she wanted what West offered. Wanted what they could have together, it was a matter of deciding how she'd go after it. Shaye had come over last night and they'd spent the evening plotting and planning. No alcohol. The one thing they both agreed on was that Kelsey had to do some grand public gesture. Well, as public as a show of her intentions in front of their friends. Today seemed to be the perfect choice for that.

Everyone was getting together at the Moreland house for Coop and Zac's birthdays. Kelsey had known the Moreland twins since kindergarten, and it still boggled her mind to think they were born on different days. Coop's birthday was today, while Zac's was tomorrow. It would be more bizarre if they were identical, but being fraternal twins meant the separate birth dates worked for them.

A horn blasted out front and Kelsey quickly scooped up her bag and headed outside. Shaye waited in her car—the cute little convertible she was going to have to sell now that she was unemployed.

"Hey," Kelsey said as she slid into the passenger seat. "It's a shame you're selling this thing. I'll miss our summer drives to the beach."

Shaye leaned forward to look through the windshield at the overcast sky. "Nothing like the long winter months and unemployment to show you the folly of driving a topless way-above-my-new-budget vehicle."

"You still haven't heard about those two jobs you went for this week?" Kelsey asked.

"It's Saturday. They're not going to call today even if they've made their decisions, and neither of them are being finalized until end of next week." Shaye reversed out of Kelsey's driveway.

"Oh."

"So. Are you going through with it?" Shaye asked as she whipped the little car around the corner.

"Yes."

Shaye grinned. "I can't wait to see this."

"Hey. You're supposed to be supporting me in my leap of faith."

"Honey, you don't need anyone for that. Doesn't matter what you do, West will catch you."

Kelsey hoped her friend was right. She'd never been this nervous about anything. Not even the night she'd given West her virginity had butterflies plagued her the way they were right now. Then again, she hadn't known what could go wrong then. How much it could hurt to totally open herself up to someone and have them reject you. And here she was planning to do it all over again.

It seemed to take no time at all to drive the thirty minutes to the Moreland family home. "Wow. That was quick," Kelsey commented as Shaye pulled up at the kerb.

"Yep. We got all green lights. I think it's a sign you're doing the right thing." Shaye grinned as she shut off the car and reached into the back for her bag. "Let's get this party started."

Kelsey swallowed, her throat tight with nerves and strained to the point of pain as she did so. She needed to take a breath, calm down and concentrate on what she planned to do, not what the outcome might be. Like Shaye said, she had to have faith that West would be there to catch her. If she didn't trust him to be there, she may as well turn around and head home now.

WEST CURSED a blue streak as he caught yet another red light. Story of his life. If he wasn't getting them on the road, he was getting them from Kelsey. She hadn't called him. Hadn't come into work and hadn't turned up on his doorstep in the middle of the night. He sighed. He had to stop obsessing over her. She'd need time to process what he'd said and then she'd need time to work up the courage to come to him.

If that's what she decided to do.

Determined to put Kelsey out of his mind, West concentrated on getting to Zac and Coop's parents' place without crashing. The Moreland driveway and the street surrounding it were packed with cars. He had to drive six houses down before he could park. Switching of the engine, he reached over for the two presents on the passenger seat. He'd bought them both the same thing. It was a tradition that had started back in primary school. The guys were so determined to be treated as two individuals that they'd refused all gifts that were identical.

He grinned. Last year he'd bought them matching T-shirts. This year he'd gone with hats. It was stupid, and their real presents— yearly subscriptions to magazines, different of course—would be turning up in the mail soon enough, but it was something he did every year. West stepped out of the car and pocketed his keys. The walk to the Moreland's gave him a chance to look for Kelsey's car. His heart squeezed when he didn't see it. Maybe, like him, she was late.

Or she's not coming.

West didn't want to contemplate that thought. Bypassing the front door, he walked to the open side gate. The hum of voices echoed between the fence and the house, telling him the party was well underway. Zac spotted him first. As usual, his best friend was manning the barbeque. Coop, on the other hand, was involved in a lively conversation with Shaye and Nikki. West worked his way over to Zac and handed over one of the gifts.

"Do I even bother opening this?" Zac asked with a grin. "Or do I just wait until Coop opens his to see what you got us?"

West extended his hand to Zac. "Happy birthday for tomorrow."

"Thanks." Zac leaned over and put the present on the table behind him. "You get that kitchen sorted yet?"

"Yeah, Coop ran up an estimate for me yesterday. It's not as bad as we first thought. Should be up and running in weeks not months, which is a relief."

"Speaking of my brother, he's heading this way with some liquid refreshments." Zac tipped his head, indicating over West's shoulder. "About time too."

"I heard that." Coop handed West and Zac a bottle each. "All you had to do was give me a shout little brother."

Zac shrugged and continued to turn the sausages sizzling on the hotplate.

"Are we still in a snit?" Coop asked.

"Fuck off."

"Ooo, definitely still snitty." Coop grinned.

West had had enough of Zac's attitude. It was time to find out what the hell was going on with him. "What gives man? You've been a prick for months."

"Nothing," Zac grumbled without making eye contact with either of them.

West sighed. He'd tried to get Zac to talk to him the other week with no luck. Today didn't appear to be any different.

"Let's leave pussy boy to sulk. C'mon, Cassie has something she's keeping secret, but I figure you should know."

"What? Cassie has a secret?"

"Shh," Zac hissed. "No one knows but us, and you if you can keep your trap shut."

What the fuck? West raised one eyebrow.

"I'm serious, man. She's not telling Mum and Dad until after the party because she doesn't want to take away from our day," Zac said with a roll of his eyes.

"Not that either of us give a shit about that, but it's what little sister wants, and you know if someone doesn't give her what she wants all hell will break loose. Besides, she's got that Neanderthal of hers who could crack heads just by looking at them." Coop faked a scared look but only managed to look like an idiot.

Before they could go find Cassie, she and Luc walked over. West didn't need to hear a word to know that whatever had put that glow on Cassie's face and the sparkle in her eyes was the best thing to happen to her since she took Are You Game? from a fledgling business to the successful company it was today.

"They told you, didn't they?" Cassie eyed her brothers.

"No. I know nothing." West grinned.

"As if," she scoffed.

"No, seriously. All they said was you had news."

Cassie crooked her index finger and urged him to lean over. West kept an eye on Luc. Last time he'd gotten too close to Cassie, the man had almost ripped his head off. Except the man was grinning like the damn Cheshire Cat.

With West bent forward, Cassie was able to whisper right in his ear. "I'm pregnant."

"What?" He bolted upright.

"Shh. Jeez, West, shut the fuck up, man," Zac growled.

He looked from Cassie to Luc to Coop to Zac and back to Cassie. "For real?"

"Yep." She nodded, her lips stretched from ear to ear in a smile.

"Oh Lord." West turned to Luc. Keeping his voice low so only their small group would hear, he said, "You better be ready to put a ring on her finger."

Luc reached over and tugged a gold chain out from under Cassie's top. "She's had the ring for months. Refuses to wear it."

"Oh." West looked at Cassie. "Why?"

She shrugged. "Wanted to be sure he was going to stick."

There was stunned silence and then all four men burst out laughing.

"Hey, what's so funny?" Cassie asked, her gaze bouncing between the four of them as she dropped the chain holding her engagement ring beneath her shirt once more. It was Luc she elbowed though.

They let Luc handle the explanation.

"I'm so stuck you'd need a surgeon to remove me. Even then I'd find a way to reattach myself."

West watched tough-as-nails Cassandra Moreland melt into a puddle of goo.

"Luc," she sniffled before launching herself at him.

His gut and chest ached with envy and he had to look away. He found Zac and Coop watching him, not their sister. "What?"

Zac tipped his head to the right. "She's over there."

West spun around to see Kels talking with Shaye, Mel and Nikki, but she was looking right at him.

"Her car wasn't—"

"She came with Shaye," Coop explained.

"If you're going over there, do it for the right reasons," Zac said behind him.

West turned his head, his eyes still glued to the woman across the yard. "Right reasons?"

"If you're going to go after her, and let's face it, you are. Make sure you mean it."

"What?" West snapped his gaze to meet Zac's.

"Don't play around like last time."

West stared at his best friend, his mouth hanging open. "You knew?"

"Of course I fucking knew. Half the time I know you better than I know him." Zac waved the barbeque tongs in Coop's direction.

"Why didn't you ever say anything?"

"Because I stupidly waited for you to work it out." Zac's gaze went in Kelsey's direction. "Then she hooked up with Bry and I wanted to kick your ass for letting her."

"You should have," West murmured.

"I will if you fuck it up this time."

"I'll help," Coop added.

"It's not me this time." West turned back to look at Kelsey, only she wasn't where she'd been. Scanning the yard, he spotted her walking his way. His gut cramped while every nerve came alive with the prospect of being close to her.

Nobody said a word as they watched her approach. West wasn't sure if he *could* speak. She was wearing a pair of skin-tight black jeans that displayed her gorgeous legs and a white jumper that hugged every curve of her torso. The neckline rolled in such a way that it drew his eyes to her breasts, which were showcased to perfection. His mouth watered and his groin tightened—throbbed.

"Close your mouth, West. You're drooling all over your chin," Coop murmured.

Zac chuckled and West made a mental note to beat them both up later.

Kelsey made it to his side and he dragged in a deep breath, filling his lungs with the smell of her. She licked her lips and it was all West could do not to groan at the erotic slide of her tongue on her glossy mouth. She'd obviously slicked some sort of shiny stuff on the plump red curves because they'd looked wet and tempting before she'd nervously flicked her tongue across them. And she was nervous. He could see it in the way she twisted her fingers together in front of her, in the way her eyes kept darting away from him.

Wanting to put an end to the awkward silence, West cleared his throat before speaking. "Hey."

"Hi. You were late."

She'd noticed his arrival? He'd take that as a good sign. Although she could have been dreading him showing up as much as antici-pating it. "Yeah, traffic sucked and I think I got every red light between here and home."

"You've been getting a lot of those," Kelsey murmured.

West leaned toward her. "What?"

"Red lights."

"Red lights?"

"Yeah, you know. The opposite of green. You've had to stop a lot lately."

Was she referring to them?

"It would be nice to be able to move forward without having to stop, don't you think?" Kelsey's gaze held his.

She had to be talking about them. Surely this slightly bizarre discussion wasn't about traffic lights. "Um, yeah, it would."

"Maybe you won't get any more red lights."

Either he was getting his wires completely crossed or she was trying to give him a green light. He was done with cryptic though. He wanted everything out in the open, no more confusion or second-guessing or assuming. "What are we talking about, Kels?"

Her gaze darted either side of him before meeting his once more. "We start now. No more stopping."

West's heart stopped. Then it kicked back in at double speed. "Are you sure?" He pointed to Cassie and Luc who were locked in an embrace. Their gazes were glued to each other and that told anyone who looked they were together and deeply in love. "I want that, Kels. I want it all."

She kept her eyes on his. "I know."

"I'm not pussyfooting around this time. I want forever."

Kelsey licked her lips and swallowed. "I want that too. With you."

Everything inside him stilled. "Tell me what you want."

"I want to marry you. Make babies with you. Make a life with you. Grow old with you."

"Shit. Did she just propose?" Coop asked.

West grinned. "Yeah, I think she did." She'd surprised him and everyone else with her public declaration, but he wasn't about to leave her dangling. He reached for her hands and wove their fingers together. Pulling her in close, he said, "I've waited a lifetime for you. I want to spend the rest of my lifetime—our lifetime—making up for every second that we've missed."

Her eyes sparkled with moisture, but the smile stretching across her face told him they were happy tears. "You'll marry me?" she asked.

He laughed. "I'll marry you tomorrow if that's what you want."

"When doesn't matter as long as it's soon. I love you whether we're married or not."

It was all he needed to hear. He dipped his head and took her mouth with his.

West didn't let her up for air until he'd had his fill. He'd missed this. Touching her. Tasting her. And he wanted to be sure he never did again. Pulling his mouth from hers, he stared into her eyes. "Move in with me. Today. I don't want to wait another second to start. Not now you've given me the green light." He grinned.

Kelsey smiled, but they were surrounded before she could answer him. Everyone spoke at once, and West couldn't make head or tails of any of it, but he didn't care. In his arms was the woman he'd dreamed about—*wanted*—for half his life. Now he'd get to spend the next seventy years holding her close. He'd probably still dream about her only now he'd wake and reach for her and his hand would touch warm feminine flesh instead of cold night air.

"Say yes," he said over the noise of all their friends.

"Yes."

The grin on his face got bigger. "Again."

"Yes."

He leaned over and brushed his lips over hers. "Again."

"Yes. Yes. Yes."

KELSEY SAT in West's lap, snuggled up close and watched the fire dance. Hours ago, Zac or Coop, she couldn't remember which, had dragged out the old metal drum fire pit they used to take to the beach for bonfire nights and lit it. A lot of people had gone home when the sun went down. All that remained were Shaye, West, herself and the full contingent of Morelands, including Cassie's fiancé Luc. It seemed she and West weren't the only ones getting married.

She still couldn't believe she'd asked him. Or that he wanted her to move in with him right away. Neither of those things frightened her the way they would have less than a week ago. Hell, two days ago, she would have been running for the hills. Now she was reaching for his hand. It was amazing how freeing it was to trust West—to trust what she felt for him.

"You okay? Not cold?" West murmured into her hair.

"No, I'm good."

"We can go whenever you're ready."

"I'm happy to stay as long as you want," she said, tilting her head back to look up at him.

"What I want is to take you home and toss you on *our* bed." He grinned and waggled his eyebrows, making her laugh.

"Another one bites the dust," someone sang from the other side of the fire.

"Yeah, they're dropping like flies. First Cassie, then Dan, now West." Zac scanned the people surrounding the fire until his gaze landed on Coop. "So who's next?"

"Not me," answered Toby, the next Moreland brother up from the twins.

The oldest Moreland, Damian, shook his head. "Don't look at me."

Adam, the brother between Damian and Toby, laughed. "I'd need to leave the office and actually lay eyes on a woman who, one, isn't employed by me, and two, isn't family."

Zac grinned. "My money's on Coop as the next to fall."

"You're going to bet on who finds love next?" Cassie asked, shaking her head at her brother.

"Yep. Who's in? I'm putting twenty on Coop," Zac said.

West chuckled. "I think that's a sucker's bet."

Everyone turned to look at Coop where he was leaning close to

Shaye, whispering in her ear. Kelsey had to agree with West. Coop and Shaye already seemed to be a done deal.

Coop turned towards them. "I'll put fifty on Zac. He'll be the next to fall."

"What?" Zac laughed. "What a croc of shit. I'm not interested in hitching myself up with a ball and chain."

"And you think I was?" Cassie asked. "Jeez, ask Luc what a challenge it was to get me to fall."

"It was worth every torturous second of it," Luc said.

"Brown nose," Zac murmured.

"You just wait. Take my advice and never bet against a heart my friend," Luc said.

"Yeah, everyone knows hearts are wild, big brother," Cassie added.

"You'd need one to bet against," Zac mumbled.

Kelsey was pretty sure no one but her and West had heard him, and she raised her eyebrow in question. West leaned forward to whisper in her ear.

"I think he's tangled with someone already. I get the impression she's not falling at his feet the way women usually do."

Kelsey looked back at Zac but the firelight proved too little for her to study him closely. Besides, it was getting late and she was starting to get cold. "As much as I'd like to dissect our friend's love life, and really, I don't, I think it's time we headed home."

"You're right." West got to his feet, Kelsey still held in his arms. "We're going to love ya and leave ya, people."

When West started to walk without putting her down, Kelsey wiggled and gave a token protest. "Put me down. I'm too heavy to carry."

"Kels, you're lighter than a pot of curry and I'm not stopping now. You gave me a green light and I'll poke my eyes out if I have to to avoid seeing another red one."

EPILOGUE

Two months later

Kelsey sucked in a breath as she smoothed her hands down the front of her white dress and grinned at her reflection. It wasn't the satin and lace extravaganza she'd worn six years ago, but she'd known the simple sundress was perfect for the beachside wedding she and West had planned the second she'd laid eyes on it.

The bodice hugged her breasts, waist and hips, and the flowing skirt billowed around her ankles, a scalloped hem adding to the summery feel of their day. She turned around to look over her shoulder at the plunging back of the halter neck as the door opened and Shaye stuck her head in.

"You ready? Oh, Kelsey," Shaye said as she came farther into the room. "You look gorgeous."

Kelsey twirled around, the skirt swirling up. "You think so?"

"God, woman. West is going to swallow his tongue." Shaye grinned.

"That's the plan. Just because we're not doing this the traditional way, doesn't mean I can't knock my groom's socks off." Kelsey laughed and spun around once more.

"C'mon, I can't wait to see West's face." Shaye grabbed for her hand but Kelsey pulled away before she could get a good grip.

"Wait." Kelsey turned to the dresser beside her. "I have something for you."

They'd decided against bridesmaids and groomsmen, but Kelsey had wanted to give her best friend something special to mark the day anyway. Shaye had helped them pull everything together in record time and Kelsey wanted to say thank you. She just hoped Shaye liked the gift West had helped her chose. With the rectangular box in her hand, Kelsey faced Shaye again and held it out.

"What is it?" Shaye asked.

"Open it and see." Kelsey took a step closer and pressed the velvet case into Shaye's hand.

With a frown on her face, Shaye lifted the lid. Air rushed through her lips and her eyes widened—turned glassy. "Oh, God, Kelsey," she whispered.

"You've always admired mine and I thought..."

Shaye threw her arms around Kelsey's neck. "It's beautiful. I love it. Thank you."

Smiling, Kelsey hugged her back. "You're welcome. But it's me that should be thanking you. Without your help, today wouldn't be happening."

"Bullshit. But I'll take your thank you anyway. Help me put it on," Shaye demanded as she let Kelsey go.

Kelsey took the bracelet from the box and quickly secured it on Shaye's right wrist. "There." She brushed her fingers over the silver links. "It looks lovely."

"Lovely? It's gorgeous." Shaye shook her arm to make the charms jingle. "But enough with me. It's your day. Let's go."

Shaye grabbed Kelsey's hand and tugged her across the room.

Kelsey's stomach fluttered. The nervous excitement bubbling inside her was so different to what she'd felt on her first wedding day that she couldn't believe she'd gone through with marrying Bry back then. But she didn't want to think about that now. That was in the past and today was the first day of the rest of her life. Her and West's life.

"Is everyone here?" Kelsey asked as they made their way through the luxurious beach house they'd rented for the weekend.

"Yes."

"So we're ready to start?" Those flutters accelerated alone with her steps.

"We are." Shaye paused in the hallway and squeezed her hand. "Ready whenever you are."

Kelsey gave a nod. "I'm ready. More than ready." She grinned.

"Okay. See you in a few." Shaye's hand slipped from hers.

Kelsey watched as her friend disappeared into the large room that opened out onto the beach. Out there, standing on the sand, was the man she'd loved for most of her life. The man she was going to spend the rest of her life with. She couldn't stop the smile that spread across her face from growing bigger as she rounded the corner and got her first look at West.

He stood facing the house and for a split second, she saw the anxiety that wrinkled his forehead before he spotted her. The smile that curved his mouth when their gazes met sent a burst of arousal through her. She knew that smile. It was the one he gave her when he was peeling her clothes off.

Kelsey quickened her steps. She suddenly wanted this day to be over so they could get on with the rest of their lives. Marching over the warm sand, she reached West's side a little out of breath.

"Kels..." he murmured when he reached out to take her hand and pull her close.

She grinned.

"You..." He shook his head. "You're..."

Kelsey laughed and, pushing to her toes, planted a kiss on his lips.

West slid his arm around her waist and hauled her against his chest as he thrust his tongue between her lips and took the kiss deeper. He splayed a warm hand across her bare lower back and a shudder rolled over her. She melted into him, every part of her softening as she got lost in their kiss.

"Ahem."

The celebrant they'd hired to officiate cleared her throat, and Kelsey remembered where they were and moved back, but West didn't let her go. He held her pressed against him. Their eyes met—locked. The look he gave her stole her breath. Everything he felt for her was in his gaze.

In that moment, Kelsey knew risking her heart on West again would be more than worth it.

~

WEST PULLED Kels in against his side and nuzzled her neck. She shivered. "Cold Mrs. Mann?" His lips curled up at the sound of her new title.

"No." She leaned back and smiled up at him. "No chance of that with your roaming hands and lips."

He palmed her ass and tugged her closer so that every inch of her front was pressed to his. She couldn't miss his erection. The one he'd sported since the moment he'd first seen her in her dress. "Goes both ways."

"Will you two get a room," Coop yelled from across the patio.

West took his eyes off his beautiful wife—God, Kelsey was his *wife*—and glanced at his best friend. "We have a room. In fact, we have a whole house. It's full of freeloaders at the moment though." He grinned.

Coop held up his beer. "There's still beer and food, so you're stuck with us for a while yet."

Kelsey stood on her toes and whispered in his ear. "We could always go inside and lock the door."

His gaze collided with hers and he narrowed his eyes. "Are you serious?"

She laughed and slipped out of his arms. "No."

"Tease."

"It's only teasing if you don't follow through and, West—" she ran the tip of her finger down his chest until it reached the button on his pants "—I plan on following through. Just not yet."

He groaned as she strolled away.

"She looks so happy." Zac moved beside him.

West couldn't take his eyes of his wife's tempting ass as she continued to walk away from him. "Yeah."

"So do you."

He glanced at Zac and noticed the frown on his best friend's face. "And us being happy makes you sad?"

"What?" Zac's gaze met West's. "No. Jeez. I'm just as happy about you two getting together as you are."

West believed him, but something had been going on with Zac for months now, and no matter how often he or Coop had tried to get to the bottom of it, Zac remained stubbornly mute. Maybe now was a good time to press his friend on the subject. "What's going on, Zac?"

"Nothing." Zac took a sip of his drink. "Whatever you do, don't fuck this thing with Kelsey up."

Before West could say anything else, Zac strode across the patio to where Coop, Shaye and West's sister, Freddie, were sitting.

"Zac still brooding?" Kelsey asked.

West hadn't noticed her circle back around to him but was happy to pull her against him again. He turned her around so her back was to his front, his arms around her waist. "Yeah."

"You might not want to hear this, but I think I know what his problem is."

He glanced down at Kels. "You do?"

"I think so." She tipped her chin in Zac's direction. "Just watch."

It took a while, because West was a little preoccupied by his wife's warm body tucked against him to be sure he was joining the dots correctly. "Is he staring at Freddie?"

Kelsey nodded. "He's been doing it all day."

"What the fuck?" West loosened his grip ready to charge across the room.

"No, you don't." Kelsey spun around and grabbed him. "Don't. The staring has been going both ways."

"But—"

"West." She slid her hands up his chest and cupped his jaw, brushing her thumbs over his bottom lip. "Wanna go lock that door now?"

His body instantly reacted. His heart raced, his pulse pounding in his ear—in his groin—and he couldn't stop himself from sliding his hands down her sides to cup her ass. "Are you serious?"

She rubbed her stomach against his throbbing cock. "That would definitely be a green light I see," she said with a grin.

He lifted her off her feet and grinned at her squeal. West turned on his heel and strode from the room.

"West!" She wrapped her arms around his neck. "We should say goodnight to everyone."

"You were trying to distract me from my murderous thoughts about Zac. Consider me distracted so completely I'm oblivious to the crowd of people on the patio." He tipped his head and dragged his teeth across her shoulder. "I can't wait to get you behind that locked door, Mrs. Mann."

Kelsey groaned and tilted her head to the side to offer him her neck. "Is it locked yet?"

West grinned. "Almost."

He moved through the house towards the master suite. He'd snuck away earlier to organize a surprise for his wife and he couldn't wait to see her reaction. West cleared the doorway, stopped just over the threshold and lowered Kelsey to her feet.

"Before we start and I get carried away, I want to say something."

She looked up at him with eyes full of love and his heart just about stopped. "What?"

He cupped her face and laid his forehead on hers. "I love you so much I can't think. Can't breathe. You are everything that makes me good. And I promise you, I will never let a day go by where I don't tell you I love you."

"West," Kelsey sighed his name and he couldn't resist pressing his lips to hers.

He'd intended it to be a quick peck, but as usual, Kelsey's mouth proved too tempting and they were soon lost in the hot, wet slide of a carnal kiss. West wasn't sure who started removing clothes first, but he soon found himself minus a shirt and Kelsey's dress was undone and hanging around her waist.

"Jesus. We haven't even shut the door." West reached over and flung the door closed, plunging the room into darkness. He backed her towards the bed, his eyes slowly adjusting to the lack of light.

"We need to get out of these clothes." Kelsey tugged on the button of his pants.

West put his hand over hers. "Hang on. I want the light on first."

He took her with him as he moved to the bedside table and the lamp he'd brought just for tonight.

"Let me switch...ah, there."

Kelsey's eyelids fluttered. Her eyes growing wide as the soft glow of his wedding present to them filled the room.

"What the hell?" She started down at the lamp.

"Happy wedding day, Kels." West tipped her chin up and kissed her softly.

"What?" She leaned away from him and blinked several times. "I haven't had that much champagne, but I swear that light is green."

He grinned down at her. "It is."

Kelsey shook her head a couple of times. "A green lamp?"

"No." Chuckling, he pulled her tighter against him. "It's our very own green light."

For a second, she stared at him, her mouth hanging open slightly, but then the confusion cleared from her eyes and she threw her head back and laughed.

ABOUT THE AUTHOR

Rhian Cahill is the alter ego of a stay-at-home mother of four. With motherly duties rapidly dwindling, Rhian is able to make use of the fertile imagination she used to keep herself sane for all those years of slavery. Spending some years living overseas and visiting tropical climates has helped inspire some steamy stories. Multi-published in erotic romance and contemporary romance, Rhian, with the help of Mr. Muse, spends her days and nights writing.

When Rhian's not glued to the keyboard, you'll find her with book in hand, avoiding any and all housework as much as possible. For more on Rhian –

Website – http://www.rhiancahill.com/

Newsletter signup – http://eepurl.com/byrsf

Reader group - https://www.facebook.com/groups/211469429208895/

Twitter – https://twitter.com/RhianCahill

FaceBook – https://www.facebook.com/RhianCahillAuthor

Instagram – http://instagram.com/rhiancahill/

Goodreads page - https://www.goodreads.com/rhian_cahill

LOOK FOR THESE TITLES BY RHIAN CAHILL

Doing Logan
Bondi Beach Boys
Sand, Surf And Sunnie
Shut Up And Kiss Me
Christmas Wishes
New Year's Kisses
Valentine's Dates
Secret Santa
Secret Confessions: Sydney Housewives – Virginia
Secret Confessions: Backstage – Jet

Passport To Passion Collection
One Night In Bangkok
Singapore Fling

Coyote Hunger Series
Coyote Home – Book 1
Coyote Wild – Book 2
Coyote Whispers – Book 3

7 MINUTES IN HEAVEN EXCERPT

Have you read the other books in the *Are You Game?* Series?

7 Minutes is never enough

When you're building a business as the ultimate adult games party planner, you don't have time for games in real life but that's the problem Cassandra Moreland has when she butts heads with security expert Lucas Wilhem.

Lucas is a six foot five wall of testosterone and a thorn in her side for wanting to shut her VIP party down early and she's not about to let him interfere without a fight, even if he is the first guy in a long time to get her heart racing and her palms sweating.

Lucas can't believe the pint-sized brunette is ready to go toe to toe with him. He's used to having his instructions obeyed without question, but Cassie has bigger balls than most guys he knows. The tightening in his groin and the pounding in his head has nothing to do with anger and everything to do with sexual interest.

The kind of interest that deserves a whole weekend of party games to explore.

This story features wet t-shirts, steamy sex and beads—but not the kind you think.

Enjoy the following excerpt from Book 1 - *7 Minutes In Heaven* –

Cassie clamped her jaw and clenched her fists. She would not rise to the Neanderthal in front of her. Lil had been gone only an hour and already this giant was throwing his weight around. Lillian McDermott may be her best friend and done Cassie a huge favor when she agreed to be the first to host the new line of adult parties run by Are You Game?, but that didn't mean Cassie, or her team, could be anything except professional. This was still a job. A job that could break her company's good reputation or send it skyrocketing. She'd do anything to continue the success of Are You Game?, and if it meant putting up with the head of McDermott Security—aka Mr. Muscles—then Cassie would suck it up and deal.

Taking a deep breath, she focused her mind on her job—on making Lillian McDermott's farewell bash the party of the year. Calmer, Cassie tilted her head up and met eyes as black as coal and just as cold. It made her pause, the darkness lurking in that piercing gaze. He stood almost a foot taller than her, and if she were a simpering female, she might actually be afraid of the menacing giant. But Cassandra Moreland had never been simpering or particularly female. Growing up with five older brothers had fixed that.

She drew in another deep breath and let it out slowly. "Look. I know Lil left you and your team to oversee the rest of the night, but it's me and my team that are in charge of this event and the cleanup. I'd appreciate it if you and your men stay out of our way."

"Cassie."

Her eyes narrowed. Oh, how she hated that placating tone men used when they were trying to reason with a *difficult* woman. "Don't take that tone with me." She stepped closer.

His eyes flashed. Fire lit up the dark depths for a split second before he blinked and cut the emotion—if that's what is was—off. Not one to back down, Cassie pushed to her toes and got as close to in his face as she could without getting a stepladder. Her chest brushed his and the zing that shot through her system couldn't be mistaken for anything but desire. Cassie's breath stalled in her lungs and whatever words she'd been about to blast him with died on her tongue.

Holy shit!

She sank back to her heels, but before they touched the floor, he shot out his hands and grabbed her elbows.

"Oh no, don't back down now, Cass." He used his grip to pull her back against him. "Not when things are just getting interesting."

They eyed each other for long moments, and Cassie had the impression he was sizing her up—testing her mettle—before making another move. She wasn't sure what to do or think. For a start, he was manhandling her. That hadn't happened since she was in the eighth grade and Malcolm Birmingham had gotten a little too fresh on their first date. But unlike then, she didn't bring her knee up to rearrange the giant's groin. No, she wanted to reach down and cup it.

Oh boy.

He leaned closer, his lips a breath from hers. "Do you really want me to stay out of your way?"

Oh God.

Cassie's mouth went dry. The man held her spellbound, and she didn't even know his name. She darted her tongue out to wet her lips, except he was so close the tip slid over his full bottom lip before retreating into her mouth. They both sucked in a sharp breath and Cassie's eyes widened, her heart thudding as his dark gaze bore into hers. His nostrils flared and air streamed across her face as he inhaled and exhaled in a gusty breath. He smelled of peppermint, and she was reminded of when she was little and her grandma would sneak her chewing gum when her parents weren't looking. It made her feel safe—loved—and didn't that just blow her mind.

"Cassie?" Her head snapped around to find Dan standing beside them. "Everything okay?"

"Um..." She had no clue what to tell her second-in-charge.

"No problem," the giant said as he lowered her feet to the floor and set her away from him. "We were just trying to hear each other without yelling."

Cassie's eyes met those breath-stealing dark orbs once more and a frisson of heat arrowed through her belly. "Ah, yeah, um, just sorting out the remainder of the evening."

"Right, well we're out of scotch, vodka *and* tequila. Oh, and the last of the finger food is being circulated as we speak," Dan said.

"We're out of food?" she asked, turning her attention back to Dan.

"Not quite yet." Dan watched a waiter pass by, the silver tray he carried half-empty. "But it won't be long."

"That's okay. We're winding things down anyway." Cassie turned back to face Mr. Muscles. "We'll start shutting down the bars."

He crossed his arms over his massive chest and Cassie tried really hard not to ogle the mouth-watering pecs hidden beneath his tight black shirt. When she brought her gaze up to meet his, it was to find one dark brow arched and a look on his face that clearly said he was pleased he'd gotten his way. Damn the man. She hated to give an inch to anyone, and if it weren't for the prospect of being in the house with no food or alcohol and a bunch of demanding partiers, she'd never bow to his demands to shut the party down and usher everyone out. The plan had been to allow the evening to come to a natural end, only now it appeared as though he'd be getting his way.

With no small amount of frustration and anger, Cassie added, "We'll start cleanup, you and your men stay out of our way." She spun on her heel and, spine and shoulders straight, marched off, praying no one could see her shaking. The giant specimen of seething testosterone set her on edge, the least of which was the blade of arousal she felt for a man whose name she didn't know.